HEART OF DARKNESS

Elle Klass

HEART OF DARKNESS

Copyright©2024 by Elle Klass
Published by Books by Elle, Inc.
ISBN: 978-1-951017-49-1
All rights reserved
Editor Dawn Lewis

Author's Disclaimer
This book is entirely fictional. Any characters or events are purely figments of the author's imagination. City and business names are fictional as well. No part of this publication may be reproduced, transmitted or redistributed either in its entirety or in part without the author's express written consent.

REALM WALKER

Books in the Realm Walker Series
In the Shadows
The Land of Lost Souls
Hidden Passages
The Ring of Betrayal

Realm Walker Prequel
Heart of Darkness
Soul of Malice

Other Realm Walker Companion Books
The Origin: Marya's Journal
Soul Fire
Life After Death

Realm Walker World Books
Love at Frost Bite
Accidental Ghost: Soul Catcher Vol.1

Other Young Adults Series
The Bloodseekers
Zombie Girl
Hidden Journals
Baby Girl

The Inbetween
Sier
Thraves
Canida
Provence City
Drakonia
Aradia
Verboten
Navarin

1

The lieutenant's scruffy beard lifts up then drops down as he speaks. He hasn't seen action in years, evidenced by the pouch hanging over the belt holding up his disproportionally slender bottom half.

I open a portal in his office mostly because I can and partly because he hates it. Assigned with giving me tasks, Lieutenant Berker is a stern man who lives his life by the harvester book. I'm not a harvester and therefore don't follow their rules.

It irks him, making my exit in a teal flash of light, dramatic and interesting. I'll be scolded later. My parents will hear of my antics first. Mom will shake her head in embarrassment and Dad will act concerned, as if I'm taking their scolding seriously, then pat me on the back later. Mom, like me, is a realm walker. Dad is a harvester who sends souls choosing vampirism to Drakonia.

The teal light vanishes on the flowered walkway to an ordinary condominium structure in Rubina Verboten. Its modern metal frame and flat roof match every other building on the street.

I open the glass door and ride the elevator to the fourth floor where I step off.

A vase of flowers sits on a stone table, accentuating the light green shade of the walls and blonde wooden flooring. I knock on house number 412 and don't wait long before a female troll answers the door, her round eyes puffy from tears and her pink tail plumage drooping. She sniffs to pack away the sadness and opens the door wide, inviting me in.

Harvesters send the souls of the dead to Tranquility, and the Otherworld if they aren't so pure or so good. They are also crime investigation techs. In other words, realms send harvesters evidence and they use equipment and tools to study and return their results to the realm. As the realm walker of the harvester realm, Thraves, my job is to mend realm problems before they spiral out of control, investigate hands on, collect evidence if needed, and save souls not ready *for* death *from* death.

In this particular case, the child has fallen ill. The woman speaks as she walks me through the condo. "Last night," she swallows, "he woke up with a higher-than-normal temperature and now," her voice quivers, "he can't move."

She stops outside an open bedroom. The child lays on the bed. Another realm walker is in the room talking with the father, asking him questions and noting the child's symptoms. She is Marilisa the Aradian realm walker. Elves make healing potions. Her job is to match the illness with the correct treatment.

She glances at me with hazel eyes as I stand in the doorway. Her long hair is tied in a braid that hangs over her shoulder, the color absorbing the green shade of the wall. All realm walkers share those features. What makes Marilisa unique is the point of her chin, soft lines of her jaw, square cheek bones, and pouty lips.

I salute to her from the doorway and follow the mother into the child's room. One ear open to the symptoms: fever, rash, hard time breathing. I excuse myself to search the house. It is my job to find out if the child was poisoned or if any other malicious act has been performed.

Nothing seems out of place in the crowded room and there is no need for me. The sooner I finish this job the better. The family allows me the freedom to explore the house. It is always easier in these cases if the nosy residents aren't stalking me.

I push against a door and step into the bathroom. The counter and tub are so clean they sparkle. Opening the medicine chest, several fae potions are along the top shelf and elf remedies stuffed on the bottom. A stool is tucked between the sink and bath. It doesn't take a genius to figure it out.

I start with the fae potions. All full but one. A restorative potion. I guess the mother uses it to salvage her young looks by as many years as she can. Taking out the fingerprint light I shine it on the bottle. Telltale small fingerprints are on the bottle and the lid. The other potions show larger prints and fewer. It looks like the child struggled with determination to open the bottle.

I check the expiration date and roll my eyes. It is two months expired. With a fae potion, that is serious business. I bring the bottle to the bedroom where both parents and Marilisa pour over the child.

"Looks like this is the problem." I hold the small bottle between thumb and pointer finger and shine the light on it. "See those tiny fingerprints?" The parents gasp. I don't wait for their excuses before I toss the empty bottle at Marilisa who catches it in her hands. "He drank the whole thing."

Turning my attention to the parents: "I recommend keeping your potions locked and throwing out expired ones." I turn on my heel and leave the family to wallow in their negligence. My job is done.

Light steps patter after me. "Cyrus." The tone in her voice demanding, as if I must answer to her or anyone else.

I step into the hallway, not bothering to look at Marilisa. The door closes and her footfalls quicken. "What was that?"

Bossy! Bossy! "That was me doing my job."

"That was you being," she lets out an aggravated breath, "you. Why are you such an ass?"

I stop and hit the down button on the elevator and glance into the eyes of the attractive realm walker. "Me an ass. Those parents are assholes. They are neglectful and careless. Better parenting, and a call like this wouldn't be necessary."

The elevator door opens silently and I step in, pushing the button for L1. "Coming?" I ask.

Her beautiful features marred by the scowl on her face.

2

I depress the jelly like comicay on my wrist and report in, to the lieutenant. The device works for communication among other things. It sends thought to thought messages. *The parents had an expired restorative potion the child drank. The Aradian realm walker has the bottle. The rest is up to her.*

Good job. Berker responds in an irritated brain voice. He means the words but hates how I didn't drop at his command or follow the realm rules.

Realm walkers are the most powerful inhabitants in any realm, and we are relegated to frivolous missions and don't even have our own realm. We don't even get our own homes. Instead, we have to share a "family home", meaning we live with our parents until we find a mate, then we are expected to have at least one child to continue the realm walker curse.

I slice the matter open and step into the inbetween. Any realm walker can do it, but they have little knowledge of how much power they each contain in a pinky finger and never use. I created my own world, fashioned it from the teal matter of the universe. It is here I come to escape. One wall is covered in shelves and filled with various objects I've found in the realms. All of them have a use and connection to magic. On the opposite wall are more shelves filled with books. Some commoner, others family grimoires, scrolls of ancient times. There is so much more to the realms. History lost with time.

As a child, I played sick and spent my days exploring each realm. When I got older, I took the brave step to visit the Land of Lost Souls. The prison realm. Only it didn't seem much like a prison. It had green trees, valleys, highlands, large bodies of water extending from huge land masses. Our power is a beautiful thing.

Dropping onto the red armchair, I study the spine of the texts for the next one to read. I fill my mind with magic from all the realms. My aspirations are to take realm walkers into the future, show them all they can do, but I need to be well read and versed, able to defend my position.

My finger circles the round metal object on the lamp table. I spin it beneath my finger before choosing a book whose writing on the spine is absent. The soft cover melts in my hands as I lean back in the chair and open it to the first page. It is a personal journal from a dragon queen, Myovi, the ink on the pages faint from the passing of hundreds of years.

Dragon queens held little power, as male dragons ruled the realm until after the great war. The secrets of her life revealed as my eyes scour each page. Her husband took on another wife and she wallowed in her self-pity until she met a troll servant who showed her affection. Their dalliances unknown to the king. When she became pregnant she sent a servant to Navarin for a fae potion that would abort the fetus.

The servant was caught and executed, but not before blurting everything in fear of death. I squirm at the method of execution: a sharp talon was ripped across the chest and the servant was disemboweled. Myovi was forced to watch. The last entry in her journal reads: *My true love will not face death as I take my life to protect his.* I can't recall exactly where I found the journal as I'd searched so many caves in Sier, the dragon realm.

If I was a more compassionate person, I'd have felt pity for Myovi and her fate, but it was a fate of her choosing. She always knew the repercussions, not only because she was cheating on the King, but hybrids weren't welcome. Some existed and hid, most were banished to Lols, the prison realm.

In the current age, subspecies can't travel from realm to realm. They have a single passport on their chests that ties them to their birth and subspecies realm. It hasn't stopped hybrids from being born. The only ones who can legally travel from realm to realm are realm walkers. We were created for that purpose. A passport for each realm imprinted on our chests after we enter and exit a realm for the first time.

Stuffing the book onto the shelf, I grab the bag lying beside the table and unzip the matter, leaving my inbetween world and entering Thraves. I'm not happy with my lot in life but have acquaintances. Calling them friends would be an overstatement. Metford, a young harvester and beginning fledgling instructor in the art of harvesting, is one of those acquaintances. His legs hang over the cliff as I stride toward him.

Chestnut hair flows over his back, the sleeves of his plaid button-up shirt rolled to his elbows. I sit next to him, my legs dangling over the cliff with his. Chilly air sweeps over us and a dusting of snow covers the higher peaks of the realm. The drop isn't far before the valley rises into more midland mountains. The range spreads for miles. Slanted trees with sparse leaves dot the landscape. The sun setting, purple and pink break through the gray daytime sky and spread, giving way to shades of red and gold. Birds fly over the mountains, settling in the valley for the evening.

I unzip my bag and pull out a drink made from the hops of Canida. One of the best perks to being a realm walker is the ability to not only go to any realm but to go anywhere in any realm. Canida is the realm of the lycans, powerful and large wolves, and their alcoholic beverages are made for large people, meaning we only need one a piece to feel the buzz. Two and we'd be stumbling home.

He takes the drink from my hand. "I successfully walked my first fledgling through harvesting their first soul today," he says without joy, unscrewing the lid. "A child. He died of a disease that caused festering blisters all over his little body." He takes a large gulp followed by a second before he drops the drink between his legs. I think maybe today should have been a two a piece drink day.

"Did he go to Tranquility?"

Realm Walker

Metford's head swivels and color swirls in his eyes as he meets my gaze. "Of course. He was just a kid." The colors in harvesters' eyes make it possible for them to see spirits. They don't harvest in their physical form but in spirit form. Not only can their physical form not pass through the veil between realms but they are safer from evil entities doing it in their spirit form.

"I saved a child, too. His careless parents had an expired fae potion in their medicine cabinet. They were lucky it didn't explode or implode. Fae potions aren't stable past their expiration." I shake my head, both hands gripped around my drink.

He nods. Our conversation gets lighter as the Canidan drink loosens our speech. I lay back on the thin, mostly frozen golden grass cover and watch the stars, the moon emitting its usual orchid shade. *We need to talk now!* my mother's bitter words filter into my head. I sit up and swallow the last of my drink. "I gotta go."

"It's about that time for me too," he responds, scooting his legs over the side of the cliff and scrambling to his feet.

"You want a portal home?"

His eyes shift as if deep in thought. Usually he turns me down. "Actually, I will. Thanks."

With a wave of my hands a portal opens around his tall frame then swallows him as it vanishes. I open another portal for myself that lands me in my living room with an angry mom, hands on her hips and a scowl on her face.

3

The lights glow brighter against the light walls of our living room as her anger heats up. "You had one job today, one job and you messed it up!"

"I didn't mess anything up. The parents' negligence nearly killed their child." I narrow my eyes as I spit the words at her. *How dare she accuse me!*

"When will you learn being a realm walker is about more than solving riddles? It's about empathy and keeping peace. Your attitude will cause tension and strife. You will bring back the wars!"

Is that what it is? The wars, the great war. It's not fear, it's control. They fear realm walkers because we are powerful. I shrug and lean my back against the wall. "When will you learn that, being realm walkers, we have great strength? If Merla didn't mean for us to use our power for something more then why did she give it to us?" Merla was the great sea fae who made realm walkers. In all my scavenging I'd never found her realm grimoire containing the spell that created us.

Frustration racks her as she paces, one hand on a hip, the other raking her short hair. She stops and spins on her heels. "One day you will take over this realm. It will be yours until you have children. Until then you will do what is expected of a realm walker," she says, her words firm and forceful. She strides closer. "Do you understand?" Her long, thin finger pointed at me.

This would be a great time to vanish into my inbetween world, but my mom has the ability to enter it, not that I think she understands that. However, it isn't wise to take the chance. "I'll understand when I no longer have to share a home with you!" I saunter past her, careful not to brush her shoulder as I march down the hallway to my room.

There isn't any love lost between us. The only reason she had a child was to carry on the realm walker curse. The eldest born to a realm walker will be a realm walker. My parents never had another child, proving I was born of necessity. I don't keep much in my room. Its blank walls stare at me from the bed where I lie tossing a ball into the air and catching it. The power behind my throw so powerful it hits the ceiling.

Homes in Thraves are carved into the mountains, or wooden structures on the mountains. Ours is inside the mountain. We have homes above us, beside us, and below us. Surrounded. We don't even have a window. My anger boils every time I think about it. We are of so little consequence we don't even get a window and a midland view. This can't possibly be the vision for beings as powerful as we. There has to be more.

Each realm gave up a sacrifice and a hybrid. I suspect there wasn't much pity for the hybrids, but no doubt many tears were shed over the pureblood sacrifice. The hybrids became the original seven realm walkers and it is that oppression I believe still exists inside realm walkers as they bow to the leaders of each realm and are dutiful little minions.

My senses keener when my anger flares. The curtain between my room and the hallway slides open. Rolling my head to the side, my father enters. His goatee swallows his chin and brushes against his chest. He joins me, sitting in the chair a few feet from where I lie in my bed.

"She talked to you, didn't she?" I ask, already knowing the answer.

He nods. "She did. Your mom can be hard, but you're not a child anymore. It's time for you to take your destiny seriously."

Destiny? My chains. That is destiny for me. "What if I want to choose my destiny, not have it chosen for me?"

His face pinches. "I have days when I wish I was something else, or at least not the harvester in charge of sending souls to Drakonia to choose their second life. Once the decision is offered and made, the vampires portal to Lols and collect the bodies. I thought I'd like seeing life renew, but drinking blood... What kind of life is that?"

I chuckle. I guess there could be things worse than my plot in life. My father has a way of making me smile and opening up. "But we can do more. We can mold and shape. What if the plan is for us to redesign the realms or open the curtains and drop the veils permanently?"

His cheeks lift as he smiles. "One day, son, one day when your generation is *the* generation."

Your generation. Those words become a mantra to me as I hold onto them.

4

Provence is a small zone between all the realms. It is the only place that anyone from any realm can go to. Curtains from each realm open and close for the appropriate passport. Its only use is trading. It is neutral ground and magic stronger than level 2 can't happen, not for purebloods, but realm walkers aren't fettered. We choose not to show our strength but that is different than not having it.

The zone is palatable for anyone. No real sun makes it safe for vampires, the weather isn't extreme. In fact there are no change of seasons. The temperature is controlled, the air flow is controlled. It doesn't even have above ground water. All purebloods have weaknesses.

A thin circle of woods surrounds the trading posts; small open wooded structures with long tables for goods. Each realm has something to trade. The lycans are builders and architects, the elves have fine Aradian fabrics and healing serums and salves. The fae have a variety of potions, the trolls precious metals and fine gemstones. They also smith and take orders. The dragons are tech wizards. They are responsible for the comicays. The harvesters and vampires don't often make appearances as their skill sets are on an as needed basis. Harvesters examine evidence of possible crimes, and vampires trace lineage through blood.

Provence could be so much more. My mind floods with the possibilities. It can belong to the realm walkers, is meant for realm walkers. My exciting job of the day is to collect samples from a business in Sier, the dragon realm. There'd been a break in and the crystals used to make tech chips were stolen.

Leaning against a wood post I fold my arms across my chest until the dragon, Kierra, is free of her customer. An ice dragon, her white hair flows over her chest and across her back. She towers over me and her thick hands, feminine by dragon standards, pick up a small bag. She hands it to me. Her eyes like icicles.

Realm Walker

Wiping a hand across her forehead she grumbles, "This place is morbidly hot. Can you set me up with a cool breeze?"

A smile cracks my lips as I send an icy breeze spilling over her from above. "What time you get off?"

She drops her head back, allowing the icy breeze to cool her face. "Not soon enough. What do you need?"

I slip a sealed note out of my back pocket. "This is for Lamont."

She drops her head and takes the sealed note. "Is it urgent?"

I push off the wood post I'm leaning on. "You could say that."

She winks a steely eye and clucks her tongue. "Gotcha."

I can always count on the traders as I go from one to the next. A few send runners to their realm to deliver my notes, others will deliver them personally. This is the infancy of my plan. Each note goes to the young generation of realm walkers. They are my best hope. I don't bother with Drakonia as the vampires have only one realm walker. He is my mother's generation and not likely to be of any help.

The crime investigation unit is on the bottom floor of Crest. The highest peak in Thraves. It houses all echelons of the government from the chief on the top floor who is the final word on everything. Every six years an election is held and a new chief is appointed. As a realm walker, I can't vote in the elections even though I am central to extrarealm relations. Another unfair advantage of the curse bestowed on me by a powerful fae.

The judiciary team, law makers, and even the fledgling school is housed in Crest. It is my understanding that under it all is a gate to the Otherworld. Somewhere I haven't yet ventured. Blood Falls drops from the highest peak of Crest into Drakonia. As souls are harvested their blood is sent to Drakonia as life-giving nectar for vampires.

The elevator door slides open and I enter CIU. The underdogs of the realm. CIU doesn't help harvest souls and is considered the muck and mire of the realm. Their jobs are underappreciated, like mine. The bag in my hand, I make my way to the receptionist at the stone counter and lift the bag. "Is Culer in?" She's head of CIU.

The receptionist's thick lips smile as she depresses her comicay. "She's in a meeting, but will be with you soon. Take a seat."

The office isn't much, carved out of the mountain without a single window, much like the condo they stuck my family in. The CIU try to make it cozy with paintings and comfortable chairs made of Aradian cloth. I set the bag on a table next to the chair I choose and sit.

"I made a fresh pot of hyndra, would you like a cup?" Hyndra is a dark brew, its sour taste is overcome with sweet cream.

That tells me my wait might be a while. "Thanks."

A curl escapes the bun on her head as she places the cup of hyndra on the table and takes a seat. Twisting the metal bracelet on her arm she says, "It's been tense."

"How so?"

"The chief, that's who her meeting is with. I don't know the details. You know anytime the chief comes down here it's chaos. On top of that I was late again. Tate's been giving me a hard time every morning about classes. He suddenly doesn't like school and Marcer has the day shift now at the fledgling academy." She grabs her cup of hyndra with both hands.

Tate is her son and Marcer her mate. I make enough trips to CIU we are casual friends. *What does the chief want?* He avoids CIU like it's a plague on Thraves and everyone who works down here the lowest life form. "Has he started harvesting yet?"

"No." She shakes her head and rolls her eyes. "He has a couple more years before that happens."

Our conversation is interrupted when a door opens. She excuses herself and sprints to her desk. Culer strides into the waiting room. It is difficult to tell from her expression what the meeting was about. She keeps a better poker face than anyone I know.

An orchid business suit flatters her curvy frame and a tomboy hairstyle finishes her business-yet-stern appearance. Her swirling eyes meet my gaze as she nods her head for me to follow.

Lights in the ceiling illuminate the smooth hand-carved walls. All energy in the realms tap into a power source of magic that fills each realm. She closes the door behind me.

I hand her the bag, which she takes and places on the edge of her thick wooden desk. She folds her arms and studies me for a moment. "The chief just left and we have a serious problem." She stalks around her desk and sits. "There's a disturbance in Lols and we need eyes on the ground. We can only enter in spirit form. You can enter in a physical form."

"Why not give this to the vampires? They can portal."

She turns her eyes and focuses them on something behind me. "They have a weakness, you don't." Her eyes refocus on mine. "You're different than your mother and don't play by the rules. The chief has noticed that and," she shrugs, "that's why he chose you."

REALM WALKER

Is my job about to get exciting? "What is it you need me to do?"

5

It isn't a one-day job, and takes me to Lols. Of course, I accept, and being chief's orders I won't be tasked with any everyday menial assignments until this problem is solved. The seeds planted, I have realm walker business to take care of first.

The new generation of realm walkers enters Provence. All of us aged closely with a gap of no more than five years. A bustling trade center during the day, at night it is silent. All young realm walkers present, not a single one shows an inkling of wanting to be here. Arms folded, hands on hips, straight lips, and eye rolls are all I get. They couldn't look more put out if they tried.

I am the black sheep but I'm about to open doors for them. Marilisa glares at me with her half-moon-shaped defiant eyes. Still upset over yesterday, I suppose. Of all the realm walkers she is the most beautiful and always catches my eye. The fake twinkling stars and pink and silver moons shine in every realm walker's hair as they tilt and shift. Their hair reflects various shades.

"Get on with it," Hackey calls in a snippy voice. He represents the realm Canida and has as much tact as a lycan. His long, straight, thin hair hangs over his broad shoulders. Genetically, he is very much a lycan and as tall as any.

I step to the middle of the semi-circle they form. "What did any of you do today?"

Mumbles and confused faces bounce between them before Marilisa speaks up. "We saved a life together yesterday." Her words concise, arms folded across her chest.

I pull my lips into a smile. "That was a ridiculous call. They didn't need us." I meet the gaze of each one. "How many of you go on calls that could be taken care of without you?"

Murmurs sweep over them as they glance at one another. Lamont clears his throat, quieting the mumbles. "Never. Most problems can be solved in another way, but this is our job." The tension in his voice makes it obvious to me he isn't overly pleased with his lot in life either. As the dragon realm walker, genetically he is very much dragon and as tall as Hackey only bigger boned with a prominent layer of fat, quite normal for those who live in the cold year-round. Dragons and lycans are evolutionary cousins. His hair buzzed short; his entire scalp moves when he speaks.

"Anyone else?"

Jine the realm walker of Verboten glances at each of the others then stares at me. The shortest of us all, she stands a near half a meter under Hackey and Lamont, but that doesn't stop her. Her gaze subzero, chilling my bones. "What are you getting at?" The ringlets on her head stand out like ice-picks.

That's more like it. I can count on her snippy attitude to spice the moment. I bring my hands to my forehead and draw them downward in a circle. A shield manifests around us. Each realm walker shifts uneasily with the change in energy. It is innate to us…to me. They need to learn. We can reshape and reform energy and matter but rarely, as in never, do we do it.

Heads study the shield and Jine shouts above the grumbling group. "That's incredible. How?"

There's much they need to learn about their own abilities. "It's easy and any of you can do it." They aren't all sold judging by the scowls on some of their faces. I need to show them more in the security of my protective bubble that would make us invisible to anyone who might be spying or strolling to Provence in the late night. The ground rumbles beneath our feet and splits open. The energy moves through the shield like jelly.

Gasps and eyes widened as some glance into the void and see the underground stream. We all know it's there but never has anyone gazed on it, until now anyways. "We are more than they want us to be. We are realm walkers with infinite power. None of you has ever explored that power. We can reshape realms, split veils between realms, and reform curtains."

Utters, mumbles, and whispers stop as each one focuses on my words. Inside, they know what I say is true. A few protest cautiously, like Marilisa. In that moment it becomes clear she is the reason I'd been chewed out the previous night. She narked on me. I see it in her face as she won't meet my gaze directly, her eyes flicking to everyone else.

The realm walkers form a full circle as I draw the dirt together and put it back. Gasps are uttered but no words are spoken but my own. "We can do so much more than care for trivial problems that can be solved. How many of you can vote in elections or have a decent living situation?" Their expressions and body language tell me what I need to know and my voice grows stronger. "We deserve to have the same rights bestowed on us that everyone else has! Provence is ours. It is our right as realm walkers. We weren't created to be pawns of the realm governments, but to govern all realms. To unify them."

The echo of my words halts. A stillness sweeps each of them. Hackey interrupts, his words slicing the silence of the atmosphere. "The words you speak are true. We are second class citizens, but if we rise up against the realms, how will that end?"

"In death," Shiane, the Navarin realm walker, speaks for the first time. Her eyes shoot daggers at me, but the nonchalant flip of her thick, medium-length locks rescinds everything else. The tallest of the females, she is also thicker than tiny Jine and petite Marilisa. The fae are exceptionally uppity, making her lot in life most likely worse than any of ours. Sure, the fae created us, but that only serves to drive the conceit.

My goal isn't to harm anyone, only to fight for equal rights. I soften my tone. "I'm not suggesting harm. If we stop taking the mundane tasks they hand us we can start to make a difference. We put our foot down and meet back here in seven days."

"I won't. I enjoy helping the elves and have taken on the most important task of caring for Serenity Tree. I suggest," Marilisa's half-moon eyes narrow as she studies each of us except me, "you each find a task imperative to your realm and don't listen to his nonsense. We weren't made to destroy but to help." Her words don't shock or surprise me. I nearly expect it from her but I'll find a way to turn her or won't. She can do her thing and we'll do ours.

Her words settle on the group as they mingle and discuss. I use the opportunity to take Marilisa aside to confront her. "You said something yesterday didn't you?"

She guffaws. "What exactly are you accusing me of?" Her moonlight shaded eyes meeting mine. Something as perfect as her shouldn't be such a pain in my ass. She's like a thorn perpetually needling my skin.

"I took heat for yesterday. You were there."

Flames rise in her eyes and cheeks. "I can't stand you, but you're still one of us. I'll never agree with your views and will always despise your attitude, but never would I turn you in."

The edges of my lips lift in a satisfied smile. "You acknowledge everything I said here today."

Her body shakes in anger. "You are a barbaric, egotistical moron whose ideas reek worse than yellow toadflax!" Spinning on her heel she marches off, plowing right through my shield.

The energy ripples to my core and a chuckle escapes my lips. Anger is the key to getting her to use her power and manipulate energy and matter as we are meant to do. I scratch my earlier thought. I will find a way even if it means poking her buttons on a regular basis.

Jine, Shiane, and Lamont confirm they will meet back in seven days. Marilisa is a definite no for now. I'll find a way to win her over, even if it means sparking the fiery energy inside her. Hackey is a possibility.

6

My senses overload as vehicles blow past me, honking and playing music. Conversations filter into my head, and the scent of exhaust makes the air nearly unbreathable. I squeeze my eyes shut in an effort to block it all out. Regaining my composure, I scan the street, not a single commoner notices my abrupt appearance in the heart of London, except for a child. Her golden hair in braids and a cowlick in her bangs forming a part in the middle of her forehead. She grimaces at me and tugs at her mother's hand as she points and says, "That man looks weird."

I focus my gaze square on her face and say, "You don't see me, brat."

The child's face goes from a grimace to a smile as she turns around and crosses the street with her mother. Able to manipulate matter and energy, I learned the art of power of suggestion fairly young.

Buildings made with some form of commoner made material tower several stories high, reaching towards the sky. Mirrors reflect light from some, others are filled with windows. Awnings hang across store fronts and entrances and signs label each structure and street. Double decker vehicles run along the city streets. I find an alley and duck into it.

As a realm walker, even in the congested city, I stand out. My shoulder-length hair reflects any and every color around it like a mirror and my eyes change color as erratically as my hair. My skin blends with others in a crowd. I wipe my hand along a store wall in the alley, forming a mirror. There I shorten my hair above my ears, make it dark brown, round my square face and lengthen my sharp nose.

It is easiest to transform into a troll and hold that, but in London I'll stand out more with green tail plumage. Satisfied with my appearance I erase the mirror and turn the corner onto a street and blend into the crowd. A metal cage holds what commoners call newspapers. I squat to read the headline. It is dated February 13, 2003, by commoner time. They have their own way of doing it.

In the realms we track time differently. It doesn't start or stop. We don't name years with numbers as they do. The headlines on the paper read *Iraq may have breached 1441*. The article goes on to explain that '1441' is a UN resolution and some man named Saddam Hussein developed long range missiles. Whoever he, Iraq, and the UN are, and whatever long-range missiles are, is of no importance to me. I'm here on realm business, not to get involved in their drama or squabbles.

A sudden fever of unexpected deaths swells in the atmosphere surrounding me. Souls with all shades of blue spheres are emanating in this area. A blue to violet soul sphere means the soul is one of an individual that has a connection to magic. Hybrids exist in Lols as it is the prison realm where they are banished to. Their minds vampire-wiped upon banishing and false memories implanted. Most have no idea they had any connection to magic. As each generation passes, the connection thins.

When I balked and suggested they send vampires instead of me I was met with the secret truth of the mission. The chief wants to make sure it isn't a vampire portalling to Lols for a fresh snack. It isn't uncommon at all for vampires to return to

Lols as most of them lived their first life as a commoner before dying and accepting a second life as a vampire. Blood Falls drains into Blood River which winds its way through the realm like a serpent, bending and weaving. Cities are built on it. Most vampires are content with the spoils it offers them but a few like a fresh hot snack from a beating heart on occasion. They don't drain or kill.

My job is to find out if the deaths are caused by a vampire or commoner. If they are of commoner origin I am ordered to stay out of it. Murder happens. According to Metford it happens quite often, but the majority of murders aren't of beings with a connection to magic. That is less common, which is why the harvesters want to be sure these hybrids aren't vampire targets.

If they are vampires, I'm to report back immediately. Personally, I don't care how or why they are dying, the assignment gets me a ticket out of the middle realms and I'll drag it out as long as I can before returning to the mundane.

In a city as crowded as London I don't know where to begin. The place is crawling with commoners. One of my skills, developed over and above my realm walker counterparts who have only barely tapped into their abilities, is tracking magic through magic. With my vision I can see things such as magic and the veils between the realms. I see building designs as three dimensional and every person inside as a heat blot. Everybody is made of energy.

Forming a map of London in my mind, I walk the streets until finding the street the last victim's body was discovered on. It is a slim alley between old buildings similar to condos. No store fronts but awnings over entryways. Unfamiliar with the ways of commoners I'm not sure I'm in a *good* or *bad* part of London. I've learned commoner cities often have these areas. I prefer the seedier areas as I blend better.

The buildings aren't as fresh-faced and clean as those where I portalled in but they aren't decrepit. They lack care. Plenty of vehicles whiz past the alley on the main road and crowds of people stroll and mingle. In the narrow alley waves of energy vibrate in the air, targeting each of my nerve endings.

Beep! Beep! My ears go haywire as I spin on my heel to face a vehicle. Its driver waggling a hand at me to move. Stepping to the side the small blue car drives past me, right through the energy stream. Tiny bits stick to the vehicle like slime and stretch. I follow the energy with my eyes. It thins as the car drives further away.

Returning to the strong energy waves, sunlight beats down on the alley even though the air is chilly. An object shines, reflecting the sun's beams. I lean down and collect it, holding it between my thumb and pointer finger. It's a long, narrow tube made of a light, shiny metal such as silver. My mind flips through pages of stored memory of commoner weapons.

They are an unusually brutal subspecies. The pages in my mind stop as they find what they are searching for. Guns and bullets. Commoners have strange weapons that discharge oblong metal objects they call bullets. The bullets are housed in an oblong casing like the one I hold. Generally, casings aren't silver, they're aluminum, a similar shade. My next step is to determine if the casing is silver which means it is designed to kill a lycan hybrid.

Commoners store books and information in libraries, as do we. My mind map doesn't specify individual buildings, that happens as I learn areas and note them. Commoners flag down and get into the seats of vehicles with yellow lighted signs above the windshield. I assume these are a type of public transport and take my chance on flagging one down.

I've never ridden in a commoner vehicle. The seat is comfortable enough but made of a strange fabric that isn't soft to the touch. It's certainly not Aradian. "The nearest library," I respond after the driver with a shiny bald head and black framed circular glasses asks where I want to go.

Realm Walker

His full lips curl in a smile under his bushy mustache. "You aren't from London," he says with a strong accent and points out the windshield towards a semi-extravagant building across the street, with steps leading to three arches: a window in the middle arch and a door under the other two. The glass in the windows has a similar arched pattern. "As fine a library as any."

I thank him before stepping onto the street, dodging vehicles I cross it and walk up the steps. Pushing the door open sweet, grassy, earthy aromas blast my nose mingling with a hint of musk. I blink rapidly as the strong aromas bring tears to my eyes.

The walls hold shelves of books beneath the curve-topped windows. Long tables and chairs fill the open space. I walk up and down the shelves of books trying to make rhyme or reason of them. Each has a label with a letter/number combination. Rows and shelves are titled as fiction and nonfiction and various types of each. I cup my hands over my head in frustration. How does anyone find anything in one of these places?

"Can I help you?" asks a timid female voice. I turn my head and meet the gaze of a blonde-headed woman, her hair tied back in a ponytail and wearing a knee-length blue dress that doesn't accentuate her tiny frame but distracts from it. "You seem lost."

You could say that. I don't mince words with the attractive, yet wallflower, young lady, "I'm in need of something that will tell me how to test metals to tell one from another."

She smiles, her lips wider than they appear under her stubby nose. "You're in our fiction section. You need nonfiction."

She continues talking as I tune out. We move to the other side of the library and through various rows of books before she stops and points downward. "You should find what you're looking for here. If you need any other help I'll be at that desk," she points, her voice not as strongly accented as the man in the transport vehicle.

Skimming through the books, I find it. There are several ways to test silver; the ice cube, ring, magnet, bleach, and acid tests. Packing the information into my brain I close the book and re-shelve it.

7

Clearing the table in my inbetween room, I place the shell casing on it. Beside it I place the tools I collected to test it. I ball my hand and form an ice cube. That is something I didn't need to purchase. Placing the cube beside the casing, it melts quickly. My first indication it's silver, but my tests are still inconclusive.

I dry the casing off for its next test. Picking up the magnet I used the power of suggestion to obtain, as I know nothing of commoner currency and passed my purchase of the magnet, bleach and vinegar onto the next customer. I looked the cashier in the eye and said 'the gentleman behind me is paying'. I turned around, smiled at the man behind me and said 'thank you'. Commoners are so easily duped.

The magnet in one hand, the casing in the other, the magnet slides off, more like drops without showing much stickability. My second test agrees with the first. My third, fourth, and fifth tests all conclude the casing is silver. The bullet was meant for a lycan hybrid.

Returning to London I revisit the spot of the energy. It isn't as bright as earlier. The faint lines show the directions it moved. Remembering how the car stretched it. One of the lines will take me to the culprit, but which one? They are like a spider web. The car drove through one of the fading lines earlier. This isn't the answer.

I close my eyes and envision my mind map of London, searching for disturbances in energy. All the death locations radiating blue, also the many cemeteries in the city. Weaker energy buzzes in and out, moves from one location to another.

I'm in no hurry to return home so choose to check out a cemetery. The energy there is different, not specifically blue but a collection of colors. It's still close to the library so I don't have to go far to find the closest place of resting dead commoners.

Vines cover the walls and ages of wear show on the buildings, statues, and large stone plaques above the bodies of the dead. Death is sacred to commoners, as it is for other subspecies. Each has their own rituals in death. A fae's body turns to dust in death, the elves bury their dead like commoners, only a plant rises out of their grave. The plant varies from elf to elf. Vampires are the product of a second life, most often offered to commoners. A dragon's body is consumed by fire, their ash spread over the land as a protection of sorts.

A large circular structure with many doorways holds more decaying bodies. It is odd how they bury them or stick them in odd buildings instead of returning them to nature. No wonder so much energy exists in a cemetery. Dead are energy, not energy that can be seen, but collections of it.

Inside the circular structure filled with doors is the collection of colorful energy. My guess is the energy of the dead accumulated. Putting my hand into the colors that rise and fall, I allow it to radiate through me, become one with me.

I listen for its stories but there are none to tell. I can't hear them, but I feel their presence. I step into the center and feel their energy move through me as death enters and exits. This bubble of energy is how they move from one spot to another.

Colors swirl around me as I close my eyes and think of the location of the second victim. When I open my eyes and step to the side and out of the energy's center, I find myself under a naked tree. A chuckle escapes my lips. The collections of energy from the dead not only transport them but me. All energy of the dead is connected.

A path, a bench, and commoners strolling and chattering as their sun begins to drop in the sky. The air growing more chilly. A pattern of colors works its way horizontally through the atmosphere. There is no shell casing or other telltale sign of what was killed, but a violet light beams from the spot of death. A single trail escapes through the trees. I blanket myself in a warm cocoon to stave off the cold and follow it.

When it comes to the street it turns and continues. I remain on its course until it forks into two violet lights, one fainter than the other. I follow the stronger one and stay with it until it forks again and again, always choosing the stronger energy until it stops.

A sign hangs from an awning, welcoming patrons. I push the door open. A long shiny wooden bar top spreads in a semi-circle with stools pulled up to it with commoners drinking and talking. The sun has long set and the light inside the pub not much brighter than the night outside. A few non-matching tables, chairs, and booths litter the small space.

I pull out a stool at the end of the bar, filter commoner banter, and scan the location

for energy. The violet energy ends at a booth
in the corner and several lines of energy
spread from it. Whoever is killing hybrids has
been here and doesn't themselves have magic,
as it disperses in the room and ends.

A woman behind the counter, the
tops of her voluminous breasts hanging out of
her shirt, with short dark hair and bright green
eyes asks, without a smile, what I want to
drink. Behind her are labeled taps. I choose
one. *Why not have a drink while I figure out my
next move?* One sip of the bitter liquid I nearly
spit it out. It is nothing like the flavorful hops
of Canida.

Images flash on a screen behind and
above the lady at the counter, narrated by a
man. The images change and center on the
speaking man, words scroll across the bottom
of the screen.

"What's your take?" a woman asks.

Pulling my eyes away from the screen,
I can't help but note a beautiful commoner
sitting beside me. Not as breathtaking as
Marilisa, but attractive for someone without
magic. "About?"

Her lips are swathed in a shiny pink
gloss making her dark skin tones darker, high
cheek bones lifting as she speaks. "The U.S.
going to war?"

Recalling the newspaper headline, and
glancing from the corner of my eye at the
large screen, I quickly realize the man on the

screen is talking about the same thing I'd read in the paper. Commoner war isn't something I care anything about. "What do you think?"

"It's not right." She turns her face away from me and appears to stare into her drink. "War can't be justified in these times. We need to find other ways to solve issues instead of violence."

A commoner against violence? Maybe I'd pegged them wrong, or at least not all are barbaric. *Is there another answer?* I don't want war either, only equality. She turns her gaze back to me, her eyes similar to my own; a green ring surrounding the light brown iris. "How can the dispute be settled without war?" Unhappy with my own life and the oppression of realm walkers, I want to know the answer. *How did one stop violence or, in my case, gain rights without bloodshed?*

"We protest. February 15th, right here in London and around the globe. The U.S. needs to know responding to violence with war isn't the answer."

Protest? I understand the term. I asked the realm walkers to protest by turning down the ridiculous assignments they send us on, not that I expect any really will stand up for themselves. Commoners organize protests. My interest is piqued and I want to know more. How else can we protest and get them to listen?

Realm Walker

I have the power in my pinky to drop veils between realms, but that won't solve anything. Can I get the realm leaders to hear us without resorting to extremes? I sip the bitter liquid to appear as commoner as possible, fighting against the grimace the liquid causes. "Tell me more about the protest and where I can find it in London?"

Her pink lips curl into a shiny smile as if I lived under a rock or another *realm.* She explains a protest is a march against atrocities. A way to speak your mind peacefully, to campaign against violence and for human *rights.* Rights, that's the word. It tickles me they call themselves human, but of course they don't think of themselves as commoners and have no idea they are living in a prison realm. Realm walkers deserve the same rights as everyone else in the middle realms. I decide to stay long enough to observe the protest.

8

I have one day before the worldwide protest that sounds as if it will put a serious damper on my mission as thousands of commoners, millions maybe, will swamp the streets of London, pulling the energy of the dead hybrids in every which direction.

The pub is a dead end. The best thing I have so far is the casing. It isn't made and sold in stores, that I'm sure. Silver is specific to lycans. It is their weakness, like sunlight to vampires, and vampire blood to dragons.

Balls of energy move around the city. I focus my attention on them. Lying on a roof, I close my eyes, allowing their energy to move through me. As suspected, they are hybrids. Violet denotes a strong connection to magic, like the one I followed to the pub, but most are shades of blue signifying their connection to magic is washed out through the generations.

My senses follow them through London and search for anything odd or out of place around them. I listen with my ears to chatter, separating the conversations. Time ticks and when I think it's a lost cause the energy inside me shifts, easily traced to a light blue ball. In a split second I portal close to the location of the shift, but not close enough to reveal myself. Staying on a rooftop I lay my body across it and peer down.

A body is puddled on the ground. Another death. Its form appears small, like a woman or a child. The string of blue light fresh, I jump off the roof, safely landing on my feet, and chase the string to a building of condos or homes. Instead of rushing in I follow the energy with my realm walker vision as it descends to a lower level. It pauses there before returning to ground level and moving towards a higher level. I portal to the other side of the building and press my back against the outside wall.

A door opens into the alley. I wait as the energy string pushes the door open. A man in jeans, sneakers, and a polo shirt exits. He doesn't bother to look my way as he slips onto the street. Capturing his individual energy signature, I pull the door open and follow his footsteps down a flight of stairs. Light ebbs into the large space from an open entrance and vehicles are parked in rows. The string doesn't lead to a vehicle but a wall made from bricks.

I mold my body into the brick, stepping into the dark space. Another cool realm walker trick. We can mold energy and therefore command it to do as we please. Creating a light, my eyes fall on a menagerie of weapons: large and small guns, various types of bullets, a compound bow and arrows.

Without touching anything, I examine them with my other senses. Arrows dipped in weak blood. My untrained nose can't determine if it is lycan, vampire, or both. Bullets made of silver, and others made of different metals, are in stacked boxes. Some appear made of a darker metal, iron maybe, others appear to be normal bullets. These are weapons to not only kill lycan hybrids but vampires, dragons, and fae hybrids too. The fae are highly allergic to iron.

Every subspecies has a weakness. There are two known ways to kill a vampire; sunlight and a lycan bite. Silver is known to kill lycans. The normal bullets can easily kill a troll or elf hybrid, but would only serve to slow down a vampire or lycan, and would be useless to a commoner whose speed is on slow motion. Vampire blood will kill a dragon hybrid. Hybrids are different though. If a dragon is also elf, vampire blood might not kill it.

There are other hybrids from the lesser prey realms such as trolls, elves, and fae that don't have increased speed or senses. They can be killed with normal commoner bullets possibly but, with magic, they'd have ways to repel such weapons. They are never to be underestimated.

The dead hybrid surely harvested by now, I am a bit surprised I haven't been contacted by Culer. I melt the weapons into a puddle that won't do the users any good when they return for them and catch up with the energy signature of the culprit.

Darkness has fallen and the earlier warmth is overtaken by icy air that grows colder by the moment. I stroll inside the same pub as I had the previous night. The man sits at a table with a group of three others. One woman and two men.

I sit at the only open spot at the bar on the other side of the room from them and listen. The lady behind the bar serves me another bitter liquid. This one isn't as bad. It isn't the full-bodied rich flavor of Canidan Hops, but I can drink it.

The man I followed raises a glass to his lips and takes a drink, his bushy mustache sparkles with remnants of the liquid. The woman, hair as short as the men, raises her glass and says something drowned out by the hooping and hollering of the crowd. One eye focuses on them as they swap glances between them, as if exchanging a private language, and chime their glasses, foamy liquid splashing over the sides.

The crowd simmers. Something called football is playing on the large screens. A sport they watch for entertainment. Children in Thraves play snowball, tossing balls of snow from one team to the next, gaining points if they do this without breaking the snowball. The funnest part is not breaking your team's snowball but watching it crumble when the other team hits it with their paddle. Football is different.

In the crowded pub, my senses are overloaded with all the jeers, cheers, and chatter. I focus my ears on them and my vision on the screen, making it easier to filter out the crowd. The goal of the game is to kick a ball into a wide net without using their hands. Instead, they use feet, legs, and even their heads. It is a peculiar sport. The team in red and white, called The Gunners by the crowd, attempts to kick a ball into a net but it is blocked, according to the group, by a player on the dark blue and white team, Spurs. The crowd's noise level hits a crescendo and leads my group to sneers, except for the female, who applauds the action, laughing at the men and calling them blokes.

'Bloody hell, James,' one of the men grumbles. A quick shift of my gaze, I see a mug of the foamy liquid lying on its side, its contents dribbling over the edge of the table. They each throw napkins at it, like the flimsy paper product will soak up the large puddle. I have to get them out of here. The best way to do that is give them a magic show. It's imperative I am discreet enough the other patrons don't take notice. Most everyone's eyes are glued to the screen. I use the distraction to head towards the group. A sign for a public restroom over a hall behind them. As I near their table I lift my hand over the edge of the table and dry the liquid as I proceed into the hall.

Not only is there a restroom but a door that says 'employees only' and another at the end of the hall with an exit sign. I'm feeling lucky as I push it open and stroll into the alley behind the pub, creating a protective shield around me. I can be killed by human bullets, but they'd have to puncture my shield first and that isn't happening. In no hurry, as I need at least one of them to follow, I stroll.

The passing vehicles on the street are quieter than the noise in the bar and I easily find the group. They've exited the pub and split. Two sets of footfalls backtrack, the other two follow me, close enough not to lose me and far enough away a normal commoner wouldn't notice. I turn left at the next road, my mind searching its map of London for a place I can have a chat with them. Some place secluded from the public eye. Two blocks west is a building for parking, similar to the one they hid the weapons in. Maybe I shouldn't have melted the weapons yet, as that's the direction two are headed. I shrug. That's too bad.

Entering the parking garage, I follow it down, whistling as I walk, and focus my mind. The woman with her short haircut and the man with blonde hair in need of a shave are following. Essentially, my job here is done since the task is learning if it's vampires or not, but I can't end it here. I need to know more. *Why are they killing them? How are vampires here?*

Vampires are known to come to Lols, but don't stay. Based on the commoners' weapons, they have experience killing them. I want to know more. I allow the image to fade out in my mind. They keep to a careful distance. All their weapons are long range; guns and a compound bow aren't used in hand-to-hand combat. They don't have knives or swords. Smart, since they wouldn't stand a chance. They have enough experience to know that, and after my little magic trick think I'm an everyday commoner hybrid.

Realm Walker

The lower floor of the garage is empty except for a couple vehicles. I choose a small green one and stroll towards it. They stop, staying a distance away, but close enough they see me in their limited commoner vision.

I stop before attempting the car door and pat my jeans as if I've lost something and mumble to myself low enough they can't hear. Turning on my heel I push energy around them. It envelopes them in my web.

9

I trap them in the middle of the nearly empty garage. Their eyes widen in surprise as they push against the energy shield. I chuckle as they squirm. Feeble commoners are no match for me. Leaning against the hood of the green vehicle, arms over my chest, I say with finality, "It's pointless. You're trapped."

The man in the energy bubble fumbles with something in his pocket. In my vision I see the other two halt their steps and turn around, running towards us as fast as their commoner legs will carry them. *Forgetting your weapons*, I think. "Suddenly you're speechless. I don't plan on harming you." *I will if I have to.*

"I want to understand why you're murdering hybrids."

The woman jeers, her eyes flashing in anger. "Is that what you call them?"

"No, it's what they are. You're the ones that have found your own names for them. Why do you want them dead? What have they done to you?" I stay calm, unfolding my arms and resting my hands against the hood.

"We aren't murderers. They aren't human. We kill them before they can kill us," she says, spite and hate hanging on every syllable.

They are playing offense. The footfalls of the others are nearly at the garage. "Tell me more."

"You think we're amateurs," the woman sneers while balling her fists. "We are professionals. This," she raises her eyes and searches the invisible bubble around her, "energy field you've trapped us in can't hold us."

Now that is funny. I roll forward in laughter as a piercing wail overloads my ears. Clutching my head, I rise up. Now I'm pissed. The ringing in my ears shifts my attention but doesn't weaken my shield or the energy bubble around them. It doesn't affect them either. They don't have sensitive hearing and use a pitch inaudible to their ears. "That isn't nice," I scold, bending the sound waves and pitching them back at a lower frequency their ears will absorb.

They crumple to the floor, hands over their ears. "We can play this game all day." The other two don't follow the road down but find a stairway to my left. My mind traces the wall to where it ends and finds the doorway. "Tell me what I want to know."

The two in my bubble think their companions will save them. I stop the noise radiating from the energy field around them and they rise to their feet, scorn written on their faces. "We will tell you nothing," the man says. His face twists in anger and spit explodes from his lips with each word.

A crack detonates in the air as a tiny metal bullet rushes towards me. *Is that all they can do?* I raise my hand and grip my fingers tightly. The bullet halts and drops to the ground with a clatter. Now I'm angry. Pulling the other two into my energy web I thrust them into the middle of the room with the others.

"I am not like any hybrid you've ever met. There's nothing you can do to harm me," I say, keeping my tone even.

The blonde man wiggles his hand in his pocket again. The last time he did that he nearly made my brain hemorrhage. A small device shines in his hands and I drive energy at them and squeeze. Tears of pain flood his eyes. I crush until the device is bent and cracked then drops to the ground, leaving his hand a twisted bloody mess. He holds it with the other hand. His cheeks flush with heat.

I have their attention. "Drop the rest of your toys or your hands are next and we'll talk nicely." Electronic devices and small hand weapons clink on the floor as they pull them out of pockets, boots, under pant legs, and the inside pockets of their coats. I melt the collection, steam rising in the bubble as the objects cool.

The fourth man, a bit older than the others judging by his salt and pepper hair and the small lines ebbing from his eyes, speaks: "We are hunters. Recently, supernaturals have taken over London. It's our job to keep the city clean of them."

Supernaturals. That's a new word. "Have they harmed com…humans?" I catch myself, almost calling them commoners. They call themselves humans.

The older man doesn't flinch. "Not yet, but they will."

I've never had any sympathy for hybrids or vampires – the second born – but I don't like this. "Are there more of you?" I slide off the hood of the car and saunter towards the energy bubble that holds them.

Their eye glances tell me there are more, plenty more.

"Not in London," the older man says. I appreciate his honesty, maybe we are getting somewhere.

They're taking preventative measures to wipe out, as they called them, supernaturals so commoners, or using their term, humans, can live in peace. Commoners aren't peaceful even among themselves. As the harvester realm walker I know of their wars and murders. The wasteful deaths. I can't trust them and realize I am no different than the hybrids they are killing. They, like purebloods, are fearful of what they can't control or someone with more power. I think of Marilisa's words as she said my plight will end in death.

Letting them go isn't an option. They'll continue their murderous quest and more hybrids will die. I don't have the time or the concern to hunt hunters across Lols. These hunters are the ones killing. *What to do with them?*

Option A: I bring down the garage on top of them. It is an older building, surely its bones aren't as stable from the wearing of time. Option B: I can squeeze the energy around them, crushing every bone in their bodies. Option C: I can send the hybrids and vampires after them. Too many kinks in that one. The hybrids and vampires might not play so friendly together. There is also option D.

As much as I want to, and think they deserve it, I'm not going low like them.

I study their faces. No remorse in their eyes. They are monsters who will never harm a single commoner hybrid of any kind again. I push my voice out, mesmerizing them with the energy in the sound waves. "You will never harm or kill another human or supernatural as long as you live."

Collectively they blink several times and the female coughs. Holding her throat, she sputters until catching her breath. I open a portal behind them, teal energy moves in waves and I push them into it. The soles of their shoes rub against the floor, arms out as if trying to catch their fall. When the portal closes I command it to split into four directions.

10

Culer's voice pounds in my head as I snuggle into my soft red chair for the night. *What have you learned?*

Now? I needed another day at least. *I have a lead but nothing solid yet.* I'm not giving her more than she needs.

There was another death yesterday. What's this lead of yours? Her head voice urgent.

It took her long enough. I knew about the death but she doesn't know that. *I found the casing of a silver bullet.*

I can practically hear the wheels in her mind spinning. *No sign it's vampires?*

I don't know. Do they use bullets? Most likely they wouldn't, but lycans and vampires are natural enemies and in Lols anything is possible. The rules are different here.

Her mind sighs. *Keep searching. I need definitive proof.*

The comicay call ends and I close my eyes. *Definitive proof.* I'd give it to her, but not until after the protests.

In my short visit I'd found a commoner food to my liking. An English breakfast that includes bangers, bacon, eggs, beans, and potatoes. It is the food source that keeps me going most of the day. I don't bother to use the power of suggestion to pay my bill. Commoners don't seem to notice the light created by portals, as if their weak vision can't filter high energy light.

The roof tops offer a great view of the city without shifting through the crowded streets below. The scene from the previous night doesn't halt the protesters from filling the streets as they march in the hundreds, maybe thousands.

Signs in their hands with large handwritten letters saying *No to War, Don't Attack Iraq,* and other phrases. Vehicles honk, whistles blow, screams, drum beats, and chants rise in the atmosphere. So many of them packed together, yet there is no violence.

If I can convince the realm walkers to do this, starting with my generation, maybe the realm leaders will listen. There are only six of us. If I can convince the older generation we'd have a total of thirteen. Still a small crowd. Would six or even thirteen be enough to grab the realm leaders' attention? No.

As I focus on the march below I realize something. I've spent the past couple days tracking who's killing hybrids. There are plenty of hybrids in the middle realms. Realm walkers are spelled hybrids, not purebloods. Many realm walkers over the centuries took hybrids as partners. We are essentially still hybrids. We share that connection along with the lack of support in our realms. They have to hide part of their nature. If I can convince enough of them to join the protest then maybe we'll get the attention of realm leaders.

First, I need definitive proof the killings aren't by vampires. The four hunters were armed with guns. They hadn't reached the garage with their cluster of melted weapons meaning they had more stashed in other places around the city. A bow soaked in wolf blood would serve as definitive proof. Vampires certainly wouldn't collect gear to kill themselves.

The following day I scour the nooks and crannies of London for weapons: garages, basements, cemeteries. Relentless in the search, my frustration mounts. I drop onto the steps of an old building. A teardrop cement dirt-mottled arch above a large door behind me. My senses on overdrive, a snap to my right echoes like thunder, followed by a swish that cuts through the air. A sharp pinching hits my shoulder blade.

Heat radiates through my body as I shift the energy around myself into a protective shield. Reaching an arm behind me I feel a long, slender object and pull. Its teeth embed in my skin and muscles as I rip it out. A scream tearing through my lungs and escaping my mouth. They lie! There is another. Anger boils inside me more than the pain of the bloody gaping hole in my shoulder.

My senses don't take but a moment to find the sound of shoes running against pavement. I open a portal and appear in front of the runner. A young woman with fiery red hair and curve-hugging leather skids. Her golden eyes widen as she veers to the right. Losing her balance, she finds grip with her hands and pushes upwards from the ground.

Gathering energy, I lift her small frame into the air as she kicks against it. A compound bow on her back and a quiver of arrows. "What was in that arrow?"

Her arms flailing, she tries to reach behind her. I press energy against her arms forcing them to her sides. "Wolf blood," she squeaks.

I can kill her here and take the quiver and bow. That's all I need for definitive proof. Pain like fire wraps my shoulder, traveling through my arm, and anger bubbles inside me but I have to be smart. I scoff, "Wolf blood won't hurt me. Show me your weapon caches."

"I'll show you nothing," she squeaks. Her small frame is no match for me. Unlike a vampire in a tiny package, a commoner in a tiny package isn't intimidating, only small and powerless.

My shoulder aches as I shrug and an arrow of pain shoots through me. "Fine. I'll kill you here." I squeeze the energy around her, compressing her body, not enough to harm her or halt her breathing, but enough to let her know I mean business.

"Stop," she shrieks. "I'll show you."

That's more like it. "Don't think of harming me again. My shield is up and the energy around you will crush you should you try anything," I warn.

One by one I melt the weapons in each cache. I watch her shifty gaze and actions. She searches for an out, tries to think of some way to escape me or harm me and I resist the urge to squash her as the pain from the arrow burns. A reminder she is a barbaric commoner. Even though her thoughts are of escape, she isn't stupid. I hold the power, bleeding or not, and she takes me on a hunter weapon tour around the city. "Are there any more of you?"

She shakes her head. "No, the others are… gone." Her golden eyes meet mine and flash in sadness and anger. "You did that."

The last hunters I ran into also claimed there were no more. They lied. Is she lying? I don't think so or she'd be cocky like the others. The first two I caught thought the other two would have their backs, save them. They were wrong. She's alone. "I did. Are there any more caches?"

"No, this is last one," she says, defeated as if she lost a game. Her face shifts to the weapons hanging on the walls of the room hidden in an old building.

Studying the weapons, I sniff the tips of the arrows. I need wolf blood, as she calls it. My shoulder throbs but it will heal. "Throw down your arrows."

When she does I use energy to slide them my way and lift them into the air. I'm not an expert at blood identification. I can't tell wolf blood from vampire blood. I don't trust her enough to take her word for anything. Collecting the quivers filled with arrows I string them over my good shoulder. The Drakonian realm walker will know. He'll also keep a lid on what I discovered.

"I've shown you everything, let me go," she pleads, as if I should show empathy for the lone hunter who tried to kill me with a wolf blood-laced arrow. She didn't show me any and I will return the favor.

"I can't. You know more than a commoner ever should."

I collect the bow, burning pain radiating through my shoulder, neck, arm, chest, and back. I use it as fodder to encourage my rising anger. Pushing the bow into place I force her against the wall farthest from me.

"What are you?" she asks. I don't want to converse. I need to make her disappear and get home and get medical help. My power is strong, but I'm fading.

"No, you don't want to do this." Her form small and frightened. She's no older than me. Sharp pangs radiate through my chest and back. I covet that pain and use it to power my energy as I silence her pleading words. I release the arrow and it splits the air, slicing it beside her left ear. She whimpers and drops to the floor.

It's time for her to join her friends in a portal to nowhere. "You will never harm, kill, or maim another supernatural. If you try, you will die by your own hand. Be gone!" I push her into a portal, commanding it to leave her in the arctic. A cold, uninhabitable commoner place.

Unable to hold the changes to my appearance any longer, blood drains down my back and arm, puddling on the floor from the tips of my fingers. It's excruciating. I press my comicay and call the only person I can think of. Preston, the Drakonian realm walker.

11

Plum walls stare at me as I open my eyes. I'm lying on my stomach. The pain in my back lessens as something taps against my shoulder. The fuzzy edges of sleep drain away and I realize I'm in a soft bed. *Where am I? How long have I been out?*

I scoot my hands under the pillow behind my head. A female voice grumbles at me 'stay still'.

I recognize the sweet yet tart voice of Marilisa. "You're in Drakonia. Preston called me to patch you up. You're in the minister's tower."

Panic erupts inside me. Preston. I remember calling him with an SOS, then nothing. I passed out. "Where is he?"

"Stay still! He'll return. He saved your life. The vampires saved your pathetic life." She lets out a long, aggravated sigh. "They did a blood transfusion and called me to stitch you up and cover your wound with an antimicrobial elven salve, so you don't get a topical infection."

"I need to see him now. It's urgent!" My words bounce off her righteous shield.

"No, you need to lay still so I can get the last couple stitches in." Her hand presses against my lower back, demonstrating she isn't going to let me up and I'm not strong enough to fight her.

A cream trim surrounds the plum walls and to the right a cream door. Several minutes pass as I stare at the door, willing it to open. I am in the minister's tower which means she knows. Exactly what does she know? It is no secret she runs Drakonia with an iron fist. Nothing happens in Drakonia without her knowledge.

The door opens, finally, the moment Marilisa pulls my attention away lowering her face to eye level. The hazel in her eyes taking on the plum of the walls. "Done. You'll have to stay on your stomach for the next day so the salve can take effect and you don't pull your stitches. No sudden movements," she mocks. No doubt my current situation pleases her.

Unable to see beyond her beautiful face I can't tell who came through the door until I hear the voice. "Thank you, Mari. I have it from here."

Mari as if she's on a first name basis with the mysterious voice. She stands, her waist at eye level. Every muscle in her thighs is evident through her body-hugging pants. A long, thin, breezy top falls over her waist, showing off her petite feminine curves. My eyes have a mind of their own as they study her hills and valleys closely.

She moves out of the way, replaced by the black jeans on Preston's legs. His body not as interesting or delicious to study. I quickly work my eyes to his face. His square jaw line, prominent nose, and cheekbones move as he speaks. "You're lucky. When I reached that roof top you were out cold and bleeding profusely. Without an immediate blood transfusion you would have died. You're not untouchable!" His voice rises an octave. "Your mom would have my head on a stick with the chief's permission if I hadn't helped you."

My mom, the chief. This is going to be ugly. "They know."

He guffaws. "They don't know anything. This is Drakonian business. Those arrows were blood-dipped, some in weak lycan blood, others in vampire. There's only one reason anyone would do that." He doesn't have to spell it out. To kill vampires, and the vampire blood to kill dragons or, in Lols, dragon hybrids. "Tell me why you were there and what happened."

Internally, I sigh relief, at least Thraves doesn't know. "I found a casing for a silver bullet. It's in my pocket." Whatever drugs they have me on, I can't feel it but I know it's there.

Preston runs his tongue across his bottom lip, followed by his top teeth biting down. "To kill lycans. Since when is it harvester business to investigate commoner deaths; hybrid or otherwise?"

"Since several hybrids died in a short amount of time." I don't need to say more as his nod demonstrates he understands the implications.

"And your conclusion?"

"Commoners are killing hybrids and vampires."

"When Thraves contacts you, tell them nothing. They don't need to know where you are. In a couple days you'll return good as new." He steps towards the door and pulls it open. "I cleaned up your mess, now rest." A fatherly concern to his words, as one of the elder realm walkers.

The next twenty-four hours are a blur as I drift in and out of sleep until Culer's voice floats into my head. *I need an update.*

Update? My mind foggy, I try to remember our last communication. Definitive proof, that was our last conversation. *I don't have definitive proof yet.*

Any leads? Her head voice aggravated as if she's sent the wrong person and I'm not working to par.

Not exactly. I've been following a shady commoner but haven't found the proof you need. Give me two more days. I think they'll lead me to the proof. I physically cross my fingers.

Two more days. I need that proof. The chief is breathing down my back.

The conversation seems like a dream as I wake up the next day to the aroma of unrecognized spices. A steaming bowl on a tray beside the bed, along with a glass of a translucent red liquid and a roll. I haven't moved in twenty-four hours and my body is stiff as I push up. A shot of pain courses through my back as I put pressure on my shoulder. Wincing, I sit up.

The bowl contains a broth filled with vegetables. I don't recognize them as being from the realms. Harvesters are omnivores and eat food from all the realms. I pick up the tray and carefully bring it over my lap. Once the pain subsides, I use my other arm to eat. The soup has an earthy taste. The spices add bite, making it delicious. I could eat two bowls. I had no idea vampires were such good cooks. They were commoners in their previous lives and the delicacy was probably of commoner origin. The red liquid is tart and clearly not blood.

I'm finishing off the roll when Preston enters. He drags a chair from beside the wall to the bed. "How are you feeling?"

I don't respond to his question but ask my own, "Where are the arrows?"

"Safe." He breathes in heavy and lets it out slowly. "Minister M'ra wants a word with you and it seems you're up to it." He glances at the empty bowl.

The minister. That can't be good, but is it bad? "What did I eat?"

Preston's lips curl into a smile. "Vegetable soup. Drakonia has the best food in all the realms and the most prestigious former life commoner chefs."

I am right. "I didn't know."

His lips curl into a coy smile followed by a chuckle. "No one outside Drakonia does. We are very discreet in our ways. There are clothes in the top drawer of the dresser, put them on and meet me in the hall."

Using mostly my good side, I pull on a pair of jeans. The polo shirt requires both arms and a little magic as sharp pains radiate through my back and neck. I don't bother with shoes.

Preston stands in the hallway, a few steps from the room, in discussion with a male vampire who nods in agreement, his eyes meeting mine. Spinning on his heel, Preston turns towards me. "This way."

He doesn't glance down at my feet. We walk several feet before he presses a button to the elevator. Once the door opens we step in. They swish closed and the cart quietly climbs upwards, the floor numbers passing on a register above the door.

We step out and he pauses outside a door. "Minister M'ra is very busy and doesn't speak with most anyone except a chosen few. Do you understand what that means?"

Yeah, she thinks me special. I can't fathom why. His words imply more and I catch the drift. *Be on your best behavior and impress her and, whatever you do, don't lie.*

His gaze gives me a once over and pauses at my feet. He says nothing and shakes his head.

"Try putting shoes on with one good arm," I say in defense of my free, naked feet.

With a labored sigh he opens the door. The room vacant of anyone except me. He doesn't even step inside. "You're not joining me?"

"No, she requested you alone. I'll be outside the door."

I'm not sure what that means. An eerie feeling snakes up my spine and threads itself around my chest. I choose to glance out the window at the desolate land. Sand covers the lowlands and valleys as Blood River meanders through the realm. The crimson color of blood reflects in the red sky. Vampires are especially adapted to their realm. I haven't much studied the origin of vampires but now my curiosity rises.

"Cyrus," a firm female voice carries through the room.

I spin on my heel to see the minister. A blue veil over her face and a burgundy wall behind her. She isn't physically in the room but a holocall. I guess I'm not so important to meet her in person. The eerie feeling subsides as it crawls away.

"Minister."

She doesn't mince words. "What happened in Lols and what did you find?"

Had I not told Preston? Sure, I'd told him something. How much do I tell her? "The harvesters sent me to Lols to uncover whether a recent series of hybrid deaths were caused by commoners or vampires." I look square into her eyes behind the veil and continue, telling her everything save for the protest and my discreet dispersing of five commoner hunters.

The veil over her face, it is difficult to tell her thoughts. Her back straight in the chair, one leg folded over the other and hands in her lap, I can't tell. She might be better at the game of hiding emotions than Culer.

"You will take with you the lycan blood arrows and the silver bullet casing for your proof, but the other arrows will stay here." She lifts her head as if studying me. "I'm curious why they would send such a young realm walker of only nineteen years instead of your mother."

I don't have an answer for that, not exactly. I ponder her words, not shocked they are keeping the vampire-dipped arrows. That would prove vampires are in Lols and, worse, kill in Lols, meaning they are up to more than a snack, at least that's the message it would send. Her job is to protect her realm.

It is her interest in me I don't understand, nor the harvesters' interest in me. Culer claimed the chief chose me because I don't follow the rules. "I don't always play by the rules."

She relaxes her head. "It would seem so." Her image vanishes as the holocall abruptly ends. I told the truth, yet stayed obscure enough to arouse her interest. That might serve me well or fail me. M'ra is the oldest being in any realm. The secrets her mind hold, I can only imagine. She lived before the existence of realm walkers.

12

As the teal light dissolves, the receptionist jumps backwards in her chair, a palm over her chest. "You scare me when you do that. Take the elevator next time."

"Maybe I will, seeing how worked up you get. I wouldn't want you harvested right here in this office."

She shakes her head and sweeps a strand of hair behind her ear. "It's been tense. Culer is out for heads. I don't think she's slept in days. I'm glad you're back."

I lean my arms on the counter, the quiver of arrows on my back. "Really?"

She offers me a shifty smile with narrowed eyes. "Go on back, she's waiting for you."

I'd woken up that morning with the scar on my back a tiny, thin pink line. All pain gone. I didn't wait for anyone in Drakonia. I'm not their realm walker and not subject to M'ra. I am curious about the ingredients of the healing salve Marilisa applied, as my connection to magic doesn't extend to healing myself or others.

Culer rises from her desk, her suit wrinkled as if she's slept in it, and strands of her hair billow from the sides of her head. It isn't at all like her as she treats her appearance with the utmost importance, always in a dress suit. "Close the door," she says in a tired, irritated voice.

I push the door closed and pull the quiver off my back, laying it on her desk, then dig into my pocket and pull out the silver bullet casing. "Definitive proof."

Her swirling eyes study the objects laid on the table. "You're sure it's wolf blood?"

"Without a doubt." None of the evidence is damning for vampires. The wolf blood-dipped arrows mean the commoners are aware of vampires but nothing more. The silver bullets say they are aware of lycans. It doesn't implicate anyone in the middle realms, but hybrids in Lols. That isn't a shocker.

She drops into her chair, deflating as the tension washes away. "You're free to go."

I grip the door handle, and she says one more thing. I pause without looking at her. "Drakonia doesn't know anything, right?"

Is that a trick question? Has Preston lied to me, or Minister M'ra? "No," I say as I step into the hallway. If they had said anything it wouldn't make sense for her to wait until I'm leaving to ask. It seems more like an afterthought, or she would have asked the minute I came through the door.

I have other things, more important things, to attend to. Going home isn't one of them. As night falls in Provence and the traders leave, I emerge. Jine, Shiane, and Lamont all show as expected. I create a bubble around us to shield us from prying eyes and sensitive ears.

"I turned down a job," Jine says, her lips pursed. "It didn't go well. My mom took the job to cover for my "stubbornness" as she called it and it's been tense at home."

Shiane nervously twirls a lock of hair. "I wish I could say no. I had the most ridiculous job this week. It's not even worth explaining."

Shot in the back with an arrow or not, I'm not unhappy I wasn't here to share their misery with stupid, menial jobs. Mine was educational, purposeful, and useful. "I went to Lols," I say. Their reactions curious as I continue. "I learned something. The commoners grouped together for a common purpose and protested something they didn't believe in. They were organized and marched, thousands of them, through the city and thousands in other cities in Lols. Millions maybe. I think we can do something like it." I depress my comicay and show them my memories.

Lamont watches with a curious eye as the wheels in his head spin. He's the first one to speak. "We are four. We can't even get the other two realm walkers on board. I think it's a lost cause."

I glance to the others, not to ask what they think, but to observe their reactions. Shiane is still twirling her hair and Jine rocks on her feet. They aren't sure and I don't blame them. I know we need more than four. We need numbers, large numbers, of people like us. People who don't have equal rights. "What about hybrids? If you think about it, the first realm walkers were hybrids. Our ancestors have long chosen hybrids as mates—"

"Because they had to," Jine interrupts. A sarcastic tone to her voice.

"Not true," Lamont argues. "In Sier anyone can mate with a hybrid, but hybrids often stay hidden. Their wingspans generally don't reach that of the average dragon, therefore they hide in shame as a large

wingspan is a sign of strength and well…
most dragons choose purebloods for that…
reason." His voice fades as he realizes the
unfairness and how he is too quick to defend
dragons.

Shiane pushes her full hair over her
shoulders. "Navarin is worse, depending on
the queen. Some have been neutral, others
even kind, but the current one hates them.
She talked the court into passing a law stating
that hybrids can't be out in public during
specific hours except to get to and from their
homes for work." The swells of pride she
displays as the fae realm walker melt away like
butter with her words.

"Verboten isn't that harsh, but troll
hybrids aren't given important jobs and
mostly stay hidden to keep themselves from
the self-important glances and chatters of
society. Unless they are enough troll to pass."

This is my point precisely. "In
Thraves there are few hybrids, but the ones
there take jobs that don't require harvesting.
They work in CIU mostly." I pause for drama
then continue: "They have to hide part of
their nature to fit into a realm and world of
purebloods who don't want them. They have
to pretend to be something they aren't or
disgracefully strut the walk of shame their
entire lives."

Shiane nearly bubbles over, her earlier
sorrow vanishing. "That's genius! Inviting

hybrids, becoming partners. Our plight is their plight." She drops the lock of hair and it untwists, falling against her cheek.

"Is there a realm that is kind to hybrids?" Jine asks, deflating Shiane's over-exuberance.

"Drakonia, maybe Aradia. I'm not sure about Canida," I respond. I've heard rumors that Aradia is on the verge of acceptance but are mostly neutral and pretend hybrids don't exist. Marilisa isn't here to confirm or deny.

"Enough must be willing. What can we offer them to come out in society? To face the consequences their home realms impose on them?" Lamont asks, balling his fists together in passion.

"We offer them what the realms won't give them. Provence. A realm to share with realm walkers."

Their ideas spew from there and we sort a plan to gather as many hybrids as we can, including hybrid legal experts. If we are going through with this we need to know the parameters of the laws for each realm and any that affect the realms as a whole.

For the first time since I was a child skipping school to go treasure hunting, I am excited. No more hiding, no more mundane jobs, a home of our own, voting rights, a chance to have our voices heard, equal to the leaders of the realms. My goals are lofty, but I see the vision and feel the freedom and equality.

The energy of my shield ripples as Hackey enters with two ice dragons; a male and a female, white hair pouring over their shoulders. They are tall and look dragon but I notice her smaller size, her frame more petite as if she's part elf maybe. Canida and Aradia border each other. He is thick and squat, shorter than the average dragon. It's like he read my mind.

We stop talking and watch him. "Don't stop on my account. We're in." He introduces the ice dragon hybrids who are tech wizards and supply us with a patch that goes over our comicays to block others from picking up on our transmissions.

"We are working on a way to solve the holocall problem. It's a bit more complicated but we'll find a solution," the female says, her eyes a light ice blue. Notably, she is shorter than the average female dragon.

The male hands us each a container, his brown eyes show he is obviously a hybrid, even with his average size. A dragon/lycan hybrid maybe. "Pass these out to other hybrids." This is it. It is starting. Blood pumps through me with vigor as my excitement builds. It's the first step to a free future.

Five of us, plus two hybrids, and devices that make our calls to each other invisible. I am sure it will take extremes to get

Marilisa on board with us but who needs her if we can get enough hybrids. Over the next several days we'll work to convince and collect as many hybrids to our side as possible. Hybrids, by nature, don't make themselves known. Centuries of oppression has made them secretive. The task won't be easy, but the idea of our own realm on neutral ground I hope will be enough, especially if we can build a unified central government, not to govern the realms but to assist the realms.

Marilisa, as expected, is sitting cross-legged in front of Serenity Tree. The moat surrounding it between her and the large trunk, its branches shading the ground she sits on. In the darkness, her form is barely visible. If it wasn't for the blue glow of the sarcanthum flowers I wouldn't have seen her with normal vision.

She turns her head, acknowledging my presence. I don't understand her obsession with the tree. It is a plant, but elves have a deep sense of worship with flora. I'll never understand. They are taught plant communications from birth and have a bizarre belief that long hair helps them communicate better. It's not logical and I figure it's more likely their long, pointy ears. As a realm walker she doesn't have to marry herself to a tree. She isn't an elf. It's her creepy obsession, and I hope to modify it to include freedom. I just need to tap into her anger. She is quite powerful.

"What are you doing here?" she mumbles, not taking her eyes off the tree trunk.

I sit on the ground next to her. "Talking with the tree again."

"You say it like Serenity Tree isn't alive. She's not only a part of Aradia but of all realms and all life, including your pathetic one. What do want?" she spits out with vigor and flames. The fire flashing in her unforgettable eyes. It annoys me she's so beautiful and stubborn.

"I want to know what was in that healing salve." I pull my shirt down over my shoulder and twist my arm so she can see the small pink scar.

Her soft finger presses the area, sending shivers down my spine as she draws along the line of the healed arrow wound. She stumbles over her words as if she too feels excitement and lust. That's probably my imagination and is more likely the surprise I hear in her next words. "It shouldn't be healed this much. It was a common microbial salve." She draws her finger away and I wish she'd left it there. The sensation lasts for only a second and I fight to hold on as it fades.

Her touch lingers more than I will admit to her as I pull my shirt up. I twist my arm back and face her. I won't give her the satisfaction of knowing the effect she has on me. "Then why did I heal so fast?"

"It wasn't me or the elves. They don't know anything. The salve was made from one of their recipes." Our eyes connect as well as our thoughts.

"The vampires," we say in unison, our thoughts and words uniting.

It is the only explanation. They'd given me a transfusion since I lost so much blood. Vampire blood is rumored to have healing properties. My healed wound is confirmation, at least in my book. "What do you know about vampire blood and healing?"

She guffaws. "Nothing more than you. Do I look like Preston? Does this look like Drakonia? Ask him or their Minister."

No, Aradia looks nothing like Drakonia with its light sands, morbid metallic odor of death, and red river carrying the blood of harvested commoners. Aradia is filled with flora of all kinds and colors. Solaflies dance in the air and leaves, sarcanthum flowers glow in blue, and the edges of Serenity's leaves shine gold at night.

Her words don't sting. She is right. Preston knows something. A secret he didn't share with me. Curiosity more than anger tickles the edges of my brain. Why not share it with me? Whose blood is it? Preston has the answers. If vampire blood was used, even a single drop, it would give me a connection to the vampire it belongs to.

13

Preston is the man of the hour as I summon him to Provence. It's common ground. The only place in all the realms everyone can go and sharp vampire ears aren't listening, hanging on each word. It's the only place I might get a straight answer, except for Lols, which is also common ground but too obvious as we'd have to portal.

The day traders roll out their tents and tables. Elves stack their remedies and hang fabrics into a pretty display that rivals the faes' showy potions and colorful bottles. The dragons aren't nearly as concerned. Small electronics are stacked on the table with a catalogue. The wolves are even less concerned as they unload a few items from the back of a vehicle, leaving it open for people to shop. Others are available to take orders.

Provence is a flurry of activity as traders peddle their goods and shoppers bounce from one place to another, some there for one purpose whether it is Verboten jewelry, Aradian fabric, or a blood sample they want traced by vampires.

A tap on my shoulder catches my attention as I spin around to face a young woman in a large hat that shades most of her face, her golden-green eyes barely visible yet mesmerizing. She hands me a note, her gaze flicking over my shoulder. I take it.

"This better be good," Preston says. I don't spin to look him in the face as my eyes follow the young woman. Medium height, round ass, solid-muscled thighs evidenced in her tight jeans, but it's her eyes more than her build that says everything. She is a hybrid of some sort - or sorts. I stuff the note into my pocket as Preston takes a step to my side.

His expression firm, thin lines web his eyes displaying his dismay. I meet him with a smile. "Good morning to you too," I say, walking past him towards the center.

I'm not about to get talked into going to Drakonia. Provence is neutral and this is a neutral matter.

He paces at my side. "I've had better. What's this about?"

In such a rush. Get down to business and forget the niceties. I guess that is his, or the Drakonian, way. Admitting it to myself, I can be that way too. "Provence always looks and smells the same. I can't say it's a better morning than any other, but I have a feeling today will be a good day."

"I see you're feeling better," he says, noting how I freely move my arms as I speak.

I don't mince words, down to business. "I healed mighty quick. Which vampire's blood is running through my veins?"

Irritated, he scowls. "That's a rumor."

We reach the center, passing several groups on their way to one or more vendors. "Is it? Explain how I'm healed then."

His face carries the same guilty expression a child's does when they get caught red-handed. "It was only a drop. It doesn't work the same as if they'd tasted your blood. The connection will wear off with time."

That makes me feel so much better! "Whose?" I demand, keeping my voice to a low growl.

He throws his gaze toward the Drakonian tent. "Not here." He grabs my arm and pulls me towards Sier. We step through the curtain. A teal light envelopes us and vanishes on the highest peak in Sier. Sticky snow falls from the sky and a chill tingles my bones. I'm used to cold, living in Thraves, but this is the most frigid place in the middle realms. I create a warm bubble around us.

"An aged vampire."

That's it? He thinks he's going to get off that easy? Most of them are aged. The selection would be less if he said a young vampire. "Which one?" I don't keep my voice low as I demand an answer.

He shakes his head and clucks his tongue. "I couldn't tell you if I knew."

Fine. He can play that game. I have another one for him. "I know Drakonian secrets, one is pumping through my veins. I'll keep them secret if you'll help me out."

Hurt covers his face. Why are realm walkers so loyal to purebloods that don't treat them as equals? "You want to black mail me?"

"I'm tired of pointless jobs, being underappreciated, not being able to use the full hilt of my power. It's like hiding a part of myself. I don't have my own place to live and I can't even vote like every other member of the realm. I'm not alone. Four other realm walkers are already with me and we're collecting hybrids."

"What do you plan on doing?" his voice carries an unmistakable edge of skepticism.

"Protest. We're organizing a protest. You're older, have more connections, know more hybrids. It's not a secret that Drakonia is a safe haven for hybrids and that vampires portal them to Lols for a fee in their efforts to escape the brutality of the purebloods towards hybrids."

"If any of them are willing to go along with your crazy scheme, they'll be banished without memories."

"That's why we need a big crowd, thousands."

His face pinches. "Your mother will have my head on a stick for this. Why can't you just accept the destiny you were born into?"

"I do accept it!" my voice rises in anger. "It's others who can't accept us. We are strong. We can change the destiny of the realms. We were made to keep the peace but what good is that peace if all we do is mundane jobs? Why not use our power to unite all realms and vanquish all the veils between them and pull up the curtains forever?"

Preston rubs a hand along his chin as my words and passion sink in. When he finally speaks his words aren't what I expect. "You're different, always have been. Your sentiments have been echoed throughout time by every realm walker that ever lived." His words sound as if he knows these ancient realm walkers personally. "I'll help you if you promise me one thing…no violence. This is done peacefully."

That is the plan. I'm surprised how easily the man caved. I still have every intention of finding out which vampire's blood is running through my veins and I have the connections at CIU to make it happen.

"One more thing. The vampire can't track you. They will see and hear your interactions and…feel your emotions."

14

I take the note out of my pocket once he's gone. *Meet me in Johnston's Pass in Canida outside Morry's Pub at 10 p.m. tonight.*

The woman, her eyes still burning behind my lids, has me intrigued. Is it information she has for me or something else? I have a couple tasks to take care of first. I allow the heart-pumping thrill of a possible free future to stay with me all day.

I am quickly understanding how much work organizing a massive protest is and find admiration for the commoners who did it, making it look so seamless. Thraves doesn't have many hybrids, but I know where to find the ones that exist. CIU has its own cafeteria as they are the less popular weirdos with non-harvesting jobs. I'm not sure if hybrid harvesters can't harvest, just attempt to avoid it, or if it is some unspoken code to keep themselves hidden, but I know a couple crime scene techs that aren't full harvester.

Jerry and Kini join me for lunch. I drink my cup of sweetened hyndra. Their trays include sandwiches and fruit. The CIU cafeteria doesn't offer the same delights and delicacies as the higher levels in Crest.

Jerry unwraps his sandwich as we swap the normal conversational formalities, before I jump into the meat figuratively. "How would you feel if CIU didn't have to be your life?"

Jerry doesn't respond, as his mouth is full of sandwich.

Kini holds her sandwich in both hands as she swishes her lips in thought. "I like what I do."

"Me too. It's not always glamorous," Jerry says without regrets, just stating facts after swallowing a large bite of layered meat sandwich.

Kini elbows him with a smile on her face. "It's never glamorous, but it's interesting. We know what happens in all the realms," she finishes, then stuffs another bite into her mouth.

Jerry lowers his sandwich and picks at his fruit. "I've always been a science nerd," he says in a tone that sounds guilty.

"You were taught to be science nerds. You're both hybrids." I nearly blurt the word, reining it in at the last second.

Kini's eyes grow wide. "No!" she says sarcastically.

"Is that why you asked us here? You got a better job for us?" Jerry asks, then takes a large swallow of his drink.

I lift my shoulders. "Kind of. It's not a job, but it's something that can improve your lifestyle."

"Spit it out," Kini urges as she drags her spoon through fruit sauce.

"Hybrids, realm walkers. None of us get a fair shot at life. We aren't purebloods," I say, using air quotes to the word. "What if we can change that? Take Provence for ourselves. It was created by the same spell that made realm walkers. Rightfully ours and realm walkers were hybrids first, making it yours too. We have a claim on it."

Jerry spits out his drink and Kini wrinkles her forehead. "Ew," she says, leaning away from Jerry.

She refocuses her attention. "What do you mean 'claim'? Like an actual legal claim?"

I don't know that yet. Jine is contacting a lawyer who is a friend of the family. He is one who's troll enough to pass.

"I'll soon know that answer, but we have a moral claim."

Jerry rolls a thumb over his chin, then pinches his nostrils shut with his fingers. "We can't just take Provence."

"No, but we can protest our unfair treatment in the realms and draw the leaders' attention. Shake things up a bit then, when we have their undivided attention, we make our claim and requests. Think about it. A realm where hybrids aren't treated differently and don't have to hide their true natures."

"It is tempting. I got nothing to lose except a small closet of an apartment, a smaller paycheck. I don't even have a window!" Kini says, leaning back in her chair and flinging her arm over the side. Green fire dancing in her eyes and hair standing on end as if electrified.

Jerry shrugs. "I always liked you, Cyrus. You are more like us and nothing like your mother. I'm in." I'm not the only person who doesn't like my mother.

Two down and thousands more to go. I consider my blood issue and the aged vampire whose blood is speeding through my veins and decide now isn't the time to ask them to test it. I've given them enough to think on for now. I'll pull in the favor another time.

The rest of the daylight I spend talking with other hybrids I know from my various calls. It is a mental list. Most are receptive, others unsure. I'm not forcing anyone, but the word is out and underground where it needs to be. Anyone interested only need contact me. I'll go to them.

Each realm has its own personality. Canida is mostly prairie lands, grass and flowers that blossomed out of lava flows, from the extinct volcano Naga, filling plains with sporadic large trees. Rivers weave and curve through the towns and underground water sources under pressure force water to the surface in areas without rivers and lakes. Many lycans are also farmers with the rich lava soil and grow hops for brewers. Johnston's Pass is a quaint town in the foothills. A small area of the realm.

In the center of town are old buildings and businesses made with all types of wood. The town government has its own building. A smooth log structure and stores catering to the needs of lycans fill each side of the street.

The day traders do more than sell a few items. They take and fill large orders that are sent back to the realms and healing remedies, potions, jewelry, and electronics are sold in shops within every realm. If we can bring permanent stores to Provence, people can more easily order and find shelves stocked with items that fit their daily needs. It is more productive than day traders packing and unpacking daily, bringing only what they think they'll sell for the day.

Morry's Pub is a dive bar and probably a good place to find hybrids. I haven't heard yet from the others and have no gauge as to how many hybrids we've rounded up. I don't know if Jine's heard anything from the lawyer, it's been a day. I approach Morry's and don't see a female with a huge hat shading her face. I see a shapely young woman with bountiful curves standing outside the pub with a boot against the side of the building.

Lights from the pub sign shine against the blonde braids weaved in her hair. Our eyes meet as I approach. I inspect every centimeter of her. She is beautiful in a way no pureblood can be. The blonde of her hair contrasts against the darker tones of her skin. Until this moment, I considered Marilisa the most attractive woman I've met, but this woman is something different and exceptional.

"You Cyrus?" she asks like she already knows the answer. I suspect she does since she handed me the note. Surely, she remembers my face.

I nod. "You are?"

"Ryel." She drops her boot from the wall and walks past me. "I hear you're looking for hybrids."

I spin on my heel, studying the curves in her pants. "I am. We are."

She walks across the dead street, wet and puddled from an earlier rain shower, and sits on a bench. "Do we get extra points if we belong to more realms?"

I like her already and I don't even know her. Stopping in front of her I say, "Not yet, but something can be arranged."

"How about skills? What do we get for that?"

This isn't a contest, but I like her spunk and play along. "Depends on your skill set," I answer.

She smiles, a little devious, a little confidant. Water hits the back of my head and trickles down my neck and below the collar of my shirt. I know its not an awning, nor is it raining.

"What was that for?" I ask, as I wipe my hand over the water on my neck, flicking it away.

"Turn around."

When I do, water rises from the street and spins in the air away from us, then into the sky before breaking up and falling to the ground as chunks of ice.

"Interesting." No, it's more than interesting. I've never seen anything like it. She can mold matter into different phases. I don't need displays of skills to ask a hybrid to join the protest. Nor do they need to show off their magic. She wants to show it off, create drama.

She pats the bench and waits for me to sit next to her. "I'm a hybrid of all seven realms, including Drakonia. My mother was pregnant with me when my father died. She didn't know he took a second life and couldn't believe her eyes when she saw him in Provence with his new family. I guess they aren't new. I'm nineteen years. He's a piece of —"

I don't finish her sentence and move the conversation in a less morbid direction. "How many realms have you visited?"

She shrugs. "Let me count." She taps her fingers and shifts her golden-green eyes to the sky. "Yup! One. Canida. That's a really stupid question. Do I look like I fit anywhere?" She shakes her head in dismay.

She is fiery like dragon's breath. "OK. How's your pain tolerance?"

"I'm a wolf who can change my coat colors. Yeah, it's a wolf thing. That's why we stayed here. I shift into a decent sized wolf. I can handle pain!" She stands. "What's your plan?"

"Let's put you to the test."

I know I should have explained my intentions, but I'm captivated so I don't. Six realms later I'm flabbergasted. She opens the curtains to Sier, Aradia, Drakonia, and Navarin. The curtains she can't open she can still see and walk into. Besides manipulating water, fur coats, and shifting into a wolf, she can manipulate air, land, and lightning. She is the most incredible thing I've ever met. She may even be more incredible than me.

My heart palpitates as she stands on one of Sier's highest peaks and summons lightning, followed by a flurry of snow. She grabs my heart by the aorta and is holding the reins. Is it possible this display is to show her power and might, or is it something else? She's different, her magic is different. Hybrids are like that, but most can't do all that she does.

We end our adventure in Provence. The moon shines like a light bulb in the darkness. Enthralled by her, I haven't yet asked the one question that should be burning inside me. "How did you know we were looking for hybrids?"

She rolls her neck and stares towards the static stars. "Sometimes I explore the realms with my mind and you caught my attention."

It takes my mind only a moment to understand the implication of her words. She can see and hear through my shield. Impossible. Or is it? Did she overhear us plotting in Provence? Is that how she knows? She is extraordinary from birth. No spell or curse but a natural, supernatural connection.

"What's the painful part?" she asks, twisting blades of grass between her fingers.

Oh. Yeah, that part. She'll figure that out in twenty-four hours or so. Mesmerized by her abilities, I hadn't thought that far. She's been to Provence, so she already has one passport. This is a moment I size up better as blunt. "When six passports ink on your chest like the one you got when you entered and exited Canida for the first time."

She pulls her fingers from the grass and thrusts her hands to her sides and balls her fists. "I was a baby. My father was an elf/fae hybrid. I don't remember that. You couldn't have said something earlier?!"

Sure, I could have, should have, but that's water under a shaky bridge now. Guilt plants a seed in my belly that sprouts and grows with each second of silence between us.

"How long?" she asks after the long pause, arms planted around her chest. My guilt a full-blown tree that reaches the sky.

"Twenty-four to forty-eight hours, give or take. Heat helps."

"Great! I'll shock myself with lightning."

I think I haven't spent enough time in Canida over the years. That's where she's been, and I haven't. I grab her hand, she doesn't stop me. "I have a place. It won't help the pain but it's private." I can't believe I'm offering the one place no one else knows about. My secret private room in the inbetween. A place I molded from the matter of the realms.

She winds her fingers around mine. "My mom is a bartender at Morry's. She won't be home when it happens. It can't be worse than shifting the first time, when every bone in my body rearranged. You owe me one thing."

"What's that?" I ask, ready to do anything for her.

"I don't want to only join the protest but help organize and lead it."

"Deal." She is one of us and, according to her, knows plenty more hybrids – an asset worth more than all the precious metals in Verboten. A realm walker, but better. She is a natural born realm walker.

15

The six passports ink onto her chest two nights later. I spend the night with her on a couch. There's nowhere else I want to be, not even my inbetween. I keep the Aradian heating pads, made from vengal leaf, applied. I picked up several from a day trader. Ryel's a trooper, even as she grits her teeth and screams obscenities at me at the peak of her pain.

I attempt to take her hand but she bats it away and gives me the mean eye. The one my parents learned after I was born. I wake in the morning, curled on the couch. Ryel has her shirt pulled down inspecting the new marks.

I join her, inspecting more than the marks, and notice the bags under her eyes. She didn't sleep a wink. "You should rest." I place my hands on her shoulders and inhale her natural scent.

She tilts her head, blonde curls brushing against my collarbone. Her eyes smile under the weariness and she smells like a bouquet of Aradian flowers. "I know I said unkind things and you really owed me the truth, but I like the new ink."

"So do I." I leave her to sleep after pulling the covers to her chin.

Days turn into weeks and she proves to be valuable to the mission and brings hundreds of Canidan hybrids our way. The others don't complain when I bring her into the fold, except Shiane. It isn't a complaint really, but a sneer. Ryel shuts her down with a frosty glance.

Within a couple weeks we amass hundreds of hybrids. To hide our meetings from prying eyes we decide to meet with only a few who can take word back to the others. Preston doesn't join the meeting as he stays largely in the shadows. I can't help but wonder how much M'ra knows. It would be naïve to think Preston's kept it secret.

Under the steady, dark night sky of Provence we meet. I shift my gaze over the small crowd and erect a shield surrounding us, blocking out our words and actions from possible pureblood oversight. "We are here tonight to assemble a protest." The crowd of hybrids is silent as I play the memories of the protest in London from my comicay. "For our rights," I continue, "the right to show our true selves, the right to be citizens of the realms we live in, the right to choose our fate and unify every realm. The right to take what is fairly and morally ours – Provence."

Jine steps forward, her tiny, thin frame towered over by every member. "You are second class citizens because you aren't pureblooded. You hide and hope the realm leaders won't learn your true natures. We, too, hide our true natures. We complete meaningless tasks that don't need our great powers. The realm leaders need to collaborate and communicate. We," her voice rises several octaves, "have powers beyond the pureblooded. We realm walkers were born from hybrids and given the ability to mold matter and energy at our will. Stand with us!"

"You speak big, but can you promise no harm will come to us or our families? Can you promise us we will get equal rights and freedoms?" a troll hybrid shouts from the front of the small crowd. Half a meter or so taller than the average troll and Jine, his yellow tail splits at the end in green and blue.

I expected pushback, especially from the trolls. It doesn't hinder why we are here or our shared plight. They are standing with us for a reason and it's not to walk away. They want promises we can't give, but we can offer something they've never had. It can only happen if we stand together.

Another hybrid, a female, tall and lanky with fiery red hair spits: "The realm leaders have never been friendly to hybrids, why would they start caring now?"

Heads nod. I need to do something to show them. Words aren't enough. I gather the energy of Provence and spread it outward and push. The trees around the outer edges appear to move closer as I force Provence to grow. The desert sands of Drakonia, jeweled grasses of Verboten, prairie land of Canida, green sands of Navarin, and on and on, become part of this small place.

Mumbles erupt as the ground in Provence moans and the night sky shifts. My power is the one thing I'm always sure of, a confidence I share with them tonight.

"Stop!" shouts a young fae hybrid. She pushes a strand of hair nervously behind ears shaped more like an elf's. "How does your display of ego-driven strength convince us we should work with you?"

I wave a hand over the expanded land and grass spreads. It sprouts from the barren rocks of Drakonia all the way around Provence. I didn't do that alone, not that I couldn't have. Shiane offers me a timid smile. I focus my gaze on the young fae hybrid. "If things don't go as planned, I can create a realm for hybrids. I can offer you safe passage to Lols, without mind wiping and mind bending. All your memories would remain intact."

I gently take her hand in mine. "If we can get the attention of the realm leaders we can revolutionize the realms. You wouldn't have to live in fear."

She wiggles her fingers in my grasp. "If you can create a new realm, how come you haven't?"

It is a fair question. "Like you, we want to belong to the realm we were born in and use our connection to magic the way we were intended. To unify the realms; no veils, no curtains, no separations."

"We aren't truly part of a single realm, but many. We deserve our own realm. It is our right. We take Provence!" Ryel says, her voice booming over the group. It's the first time she's spoken, as she takes a step and joins me, standing at my side.

The redhead smiles and pulls her hand from my grasp slowly, not like it's on fire but more like she's uncomfortable with the touch. I think maybe she's ready.

"Provence doesn't belong to anyone," a tall man says, unfolding his arms from his bulky chest. His pointed ears poke through his shaggy hair.

He is right and he is wrong. We and hybrids have a legal claim to the land according to the lawyers. No realm leader can claim it but realm walkers, who were hybrids first, had a rightful claim as Provence was created in the wake of the spell. The realm walkers are meant to be liaisons between the realms, not slaves to realm leaders. It gets sticky, but we have a claim and a working vision for the future.

16

Over the next few weeks, word spreads through the hybrid communities. More and more step forward and join our coalition. Ideas morph and new ones hatch as we plan a historical march on every capitol. The realm leaders will hear us, the purebloods won't be able to ignore us. Our demands will echo through every nook and cranny of each realm.

Provence's overnight expansion hadn't gone unnoticed as day traders showed up the next day to find it was twice the size it had been. Shoppers stopped and took note. Few complaints were muttered, but many questions were raised. Not a single realm leader stepped forward with an answer. The only ones capable of such a momentous task are the realm walkers. Everyone knew it, but not a word was uttered from anyone's mouth but my mother's. I assumed it was fear keeping their mouths shut or the realm leaders were plotting against us.

At home, tensions mount until my mother snaps, "You are barely nineteen years and haven't yet learned the most basic tennets of what it is to be a realm walker. You flash magic, grow Provence." Her nostrils flare. "I know that was you," she seethes.

My lips involuntarily grow into a cocky grin as her eyes flash in anger and hate. "I knew from the moment you were conceived that I'd made a grave mistake. You are why realm walkers aren't allowed to have children together. You are a mistaken product of such a union!"

The hate in her eyes vanishes, replaced with fear, and my smile drops like a large stone. It hits the ground and sinks into the dirt as my mind immediately processes her flaming, hateful words. She'd spoken words not meant to be said out loud, words she'd held secret even from me. "You said the quiet part out loud," I croon. "You were the one that gave in to weakness. Don't blame me." She didn't need to tell me who my real father is. There was only one childless adult realm walker, only one I called when I needed help in London and only one who took me to Drakonia and hid me, lied for me.

Betrayal shakes through my core, rattling every bone. My father, the one person at home I care for, rely on for his guidance, isn't really my father. *Does he know?* I look at her face with disgust and flash out of the living room in teal light to a spot I can have peace from her to gather all the thoughts spiraling in my head.

Metford sits on the edge of the cliff, his legs dangling over the side. He is the closest thing I have to a friend. "It wasn't a good day for me either," he says without looking to see it's me. Who else joins him in a flash of light? I'm the only person in all of Thraves that portals. The blue flash of light is a dead giveaway.

I crash beside him and, without another word we sit together, mulling our own destinies and paths in life for a long time before his gaze flicks my way.

I feel his swirling eyes on my cheek. "I'm listening if you need to get out what's eating you inside."

I suck in a deep breath of the chilly air and breathe out steam, then turn my head and stare into his eyes. "There are some things better left unsaid." I wish my mother understood that.

He nods. "True," he says and lifts his legs onto the cliff and stands. Leaves and rocks crunch as he walks away. Someone else joins me. I hear a few words spoken, but I don't have the mind to care who it is. I learned something I've always known, somehow, somewhere inside me. A truth I never spoke, and as long as it wasn't spoken then it couldn't be. My mother squashed my bubble with a hammer and punched it into oblivion and I am left to face it. I want to walk off the edge of the cliff and stand above the valley.

A voice speaks, filled with love, his words clear and the fuzz in my brain washes away like mud after a rainstorm. The man who I've always called 'Dad' sits down beside me. His long legs dangle over the side and I think that's what hurts the most. He is my dad, the only person in my home I connect with, and the truth of my paternity means he isn't my father. "Beautiful view. I figured I'd find you here," he says, pressing an arm over my shoulder as he sits. "Getting up and down isn't so easy when you get old."

The sun sets, painting the sky in brilliant hues. "This is only a taste of what dragons see when they fly high in the air. Imagine seeing the world from the top instead of the bottom."

"I've always wondered what you see when you portal or open the matter surrounding you. Is it another realm us purebloods aren't privileged enough to see?"

Only my father would think of something like that. How did my mother ever find someone like him?

His arm around my shoulder offers a familiar comfort, one I melt into. "You know."

He nods. "I've always known, but it wasn't my place to tell you. You're my son, no matter what. I know you. You have this incredible connection with everything. Nothing escapes you. You can transform yourself into a dragon right now and take that flight above the mountains."

"No, I can't... I don't know how to fly."

My father chuckles.

"And it would cause problems for the dragons if the harvesters spotted a dragon in their realm."

He sighs. "You're not wrong. Silly isn't it? All these centuries later and the realms are still divided."

"Would it be better if they weren't?"

He shrugs. "Times were bad, but that was a long time ago. Could everyone work together for peace now?"

It is nice to have a conversation with someone on the same page. All these months planning and I have a growing number of hybrids and five realm walkers, six if I include Preston and seven if I include Ryel as a realm walker instead of a hybrid, working to organize the first ever protest in the middle realms. I have no idea of the outcome but I can't not try it. "I think it's been long enough."

His arm moves and his large harvester hand presses against my back. "Whatever you are planning, I'm with you, but remember not everyone likes change. Some purebloods are enshrined in their customs and expectations passed one generation to the next. The realms have grown and developed but some beliefs remain unchanged. You have a gift, an incredible connection to magic. I don't think your conception was a mistake. You were meant to be. A realm walker to move the realms into the future."

Prickles work over my legs and arms with his words. He has faith and confidence in me, in my skills, and understands on some level I have a larger purpose than the menial tasks. I am the future and I will change it. As with all our discussions, he leaves me with much to think about. He is the father who raised me, but I am Preston's child. Something lashes at my mind, stings it, leaving a welt of clarity. I am more powerful than any other realm walker, not in pure strength or magic but my connection is stronger and I've always been more aware.

Ryel's blonde bouncy curls and chiseled features push all other thoughts away. I have more pressing matters than my pathetic mother or my heritage or a biological realm walker father who hasn't openly supported my plight. I've been helping Ryel connect with her magic in other realms besides Canida. Tonight is Verboten.

In her tight jeans and hooded half-shirt she hugs a large gemstone at my request. The lights of the atmosphere filter like an aurora, shining and changing. The gemstone twinkles beneath the showy sky.

"Can you feel its energy?" I ask.

"I feel like an idiot," she responds, her tone lifting an octave.

"An idiot whose eyes are reflecting the green in the stone," I say.

She narrows her eyes, arms still around the large gemstone. "This isn't working."

I sit cross-legged on the ground in front of her and the gemstone. "Absorb its energy. Let it flow inside you. Feel it warm you."

She presses herself to the rock. "I think maybe, no…yes." Quickly she throws herself back and the gemstone shoots into the air. Her mouth opens into an O as she pushes me backwards. It all happens in a flash and we roll together a couple times. Her strength is as amazing as everything else about her.

The gemstone crashes to the ground where I'd been sitting. Her face lights up and she bursts out in laughter.

"You almost killed me and think its funny," I say, our chests crash together and dance between her laughter and my words.

"I know. It hummed." She laughs more, her lips brush against mine as her sniggers dry up. Her eyes close and her mouth presses into mine. Her tongue escapes and mine captures it. Sensations bloom inside me and spread. What I feel is more powerful than all the magic I possess. I slide my hands from her back into the pockets of her pants and push her curves against me. Only thin clothing separates us.

My eyes close and I lose myself in the moment, wanting more of her, all of her.

All the time we've spent together planning and exploring her connection to magic and showing her mine. Our pent-up, raging teenage hormones in check. I roll her to her side, showering her neck and chest with kisses, sliding the neckline of her shirt over her round, full breasts. My tongue and lips begging for more. My fingers circle her pointed, hard nipples.

Her hands move over the front of my jeans and I don't want to stop. An annoying voice starts as a murmur I ignore then climaxes, not the kind I want, and I grab her arm. "I can't." I want to. Every part of me screams, but I can't do that to her.

Her eyebrows lower. "You're a buzz kill. Why not? You want it. I want it."

Catching my breath. Yes, I want it, more than all the power of every hybrid, pureblood and realm walker combined, but I know the consequences. I'm the product of those consequences. Turning her away is physically the hardest thing I've ever done. "I'm a realm walker. It's part of the curse. The first time we do it we create another to take our place and so the cycle continues."

She sits up, my arm dropping to her lap. "Oh. Not ready for all that. I think you have it worse than us, at least we can get our shimmy on."

I let out a strangled breath, feeling every bit of her frustration. I don't have words when she rises, brushes off her pants, and walks away. I can't let her, yet I don't stop her. My heart and body is a liquefied puddle on the ground.

17

What do hybrids need and how unfairly are they treated? From Sier to Thraves we collect more and more. It is a brave lycan hybrid who steps forward with the most brilliant of ideas. He suggests a central government I considered from the beginning. It's time to consider it further and keeps my mind focused on something other than Ryel. I spend time studying each realm's government. The more I learn, the clearer the picture. It won't be like any of theirs, but something unique.

No one is calling for a change to realm governments, but we want to be represented. Navarin, realm of the fae, has a parliamentary monarchy where the parliament is a court of elected officials. Laws can't be made by the ruling king or queen alone, but need the votes of the court. Thraves, Verboten, and Aradia are republics where officials are elected to represent each area of the realm and no one has all the power. Drakonia is a dictatorship without a shred of democracy. Sier and Canida are the most fascinating, as the people own everything and nothing. They have positions and jobs that benefit the whole and work as a collective. No one has more than anyone else in the pureblood world and everyone is taken care of. The governing bodies elected as a democracy that has little power. It is more for regulation.

I jot several notes on paper in the privacy of my inbetween and glance at the clear gel structure on my wrist, hoping it'll light up and Ryel's voice will speak in my head. It doesn't and I can't believe how hard I've fallen for her. The confident, powerful Cyrus who banished five hunters to parts unknown is a crumbling mess.

I attempt to push her to the back of my mind, even as my fingers still feel her soft flesh. It is in desperation and anguish I find my best ideas.

To be represented, we don't need to be part of any realm government but will create a new one in the tiny realm of Provence with a council made of realm walkers, elected hybrids, and a select elected few from each realm to protect the interests of their realm. A government building will be erected in the center of Provence, and a shopping mall. Day traders will no longer need to pack and unpack daily. Each realm will have a store.

The elected officials, realm walkers, and hybrids will have their own realm. Provence. We can live there in peace and mediate real realm problems instead of mundane, conjured issues that can easily be solved on their own. It will truly be a realm for everyone. My dad nailed it when he said 'purebloods are enshrined in their customs and expectations passed one generation to the next'. It is his faith in me that influences my vision. I will pull everyone together and we, the scourge of the realms, will unite the middle realms.

Their customs and traditions enshrined for posterity. It is time to put an end to it. The dawn of a new age. An era where everyone has equal rights and, given enough time as the realm leaders learn to work together through the bridge of the council, the veils and curtains can finally be dissolved. My concept is lofty, yet within reach.

My anger festers towards my mother and I rarely go home, communicating with my father almost daily. I hate her and Preston. Not because of what they did, but that my mother hates me because of her foolishness as if I was cursed not spelled. I see the irony, as I've always considered being a realm walker a curse.

The daggers and hate in her eyes and fiery speech concur that she thinks I am an abomination, hungry for power as a realm walker of two realms. A vile soul, an atrocity with a dark heart and malicious spirit. I can't stand to be near her.

I am none of those things. In Lols I could have killed the hunters but I let them live and forbade them from harming again. I want peace and rights for all. I didn't ask for more power than other realm walkers. In our cursed world, we know as the child realm walker grows their power increases and their parents' power decreases. I have equal power of two, although I don't truly hold more power than any young realm walker, I am simply more aware and in control. The others are improving their abilities, manipulating energy and matter with more precision through my guidance. They are tapping into the second heartbeat that thumps rhythmically alongside the heartbeat of every realm walker. I am a connection to something much larger and powerful than us.

In Verboten for the day, I'm bringing my idea to the lawyers. I take a seat on the soft green sofa, as Malcolm, a hybrid troll from Verboten, leafs through his notes in preparation for our meeting. He is Jine's legal connection. Not only the friend of the family she led us to believe, but her father. *Why can't my mother be more like him?*

Hybrid lawyers from every realm will be putting their minds together and sharing laws in their realm. It will be the first test of the tweaked comicays designed by a couple of young dragon hybrids.

If they work as they should, the devices won't record the memory of the holocall or be traceable in any way. This has already been done successfully with regular two-way communication. It will be as if the conversation never happened. Our comicays light up on time and we depress them in unison. The holoscreen appears.

Are we good? I ask Tamre, the ice dragon hybrid. I hold up a finger for no one to speak until I have the all clear.

Is everyone present?

We are.

Then you are good to go. Nothing is showing up on the comover. I'll stay with you until the call is over.

I put my finger down. "All is clear."

Malcolm, Jine's father, nearly melts as he releases the anxiety and clears his throat. "There are no laws governing a conglomeration of the realms. It is up to each individual realm to determine if something is a punishable crime. In Verboten, there are no laws against protesting and an obscure law protects it – freedom to speak one's mind. Right to privacy is the law in Verboten that needs to be expanded to protect hybrids. The only law that might be broken in the protest is disturbance of the peace, but if the protest is done during daytime hours and no violence occurs then no law has been broken."

"Our laws are similar but none safeguard, or have any regulations in order for, protesting. It's something that's never been done and therefore would break no laws," a Thraves hybrid speaks. He appears more harvester than anything. I doubt his hybrid lineage is from a recent union, possibly a few generations past. Thraves isn't home to many hybrids and the ones there hide in plain sight and mostly work at the CIU with so little blood connection to any other realm.

Their sentiments are concurred around the holocall as most realms have no laws for or against protesting or demonstrating. It simply is something that has never been done, or has a law somewhere in their history that protects it. In Navarin, of all realms, they have a specific law about the right to privacy in the home which broadly covers hybrids. They also, as most other realms, have a law against the birth of a hybrid. These laws conflict with each other.

Drakonia has the harshest laws, yet are the kindest to hybrids. They have no laws against hybrids since vampires are unable to carry and bear children. They do have laws about privacy and freedom of speech, laws that can be a problem if M'ra chooses them to be. As a dictatorship, Drakonians don't really have any privacy protections except one; the right to privacy in their home, but there is a caveat. If a deed done under the roof of one's home leads to the breaking of another law then it is punishable.

My head hurts with all the legalese, but we have to be sure we cover every base. Their next project, one we are already working on, is a declaration and design for the government we want in Provence.

Where are you? I need you in Thraves, the lieutenant's voice rings into my head. I sigh, disappointed it's him and not Ryel.

What do you need? My mind voice doesn't attempt to cover my annoyance.

It doesn't matter. We don't question our superiors. Get over here now and figure it out! His grumpy mind words attest to his bad day. I haven't been reporting in as I've been busy, jumping from realm to realm for meetings like the one in Verboten.

Rude! Tamre voices.

Precisely! I respond. I'd forgotten she was on the call.

18

I excuse myself to take care of the *urgent* problem in Thraves and, as suspected, there is nothing urgent about it. A business in Thraves ordered a large wooden display. It is so large it takes three separate deliveries and covers an entire wall of the store.

Slacks hang from the bottom row, while jackets hang from the top. Shirts are folded in a shelved space in the middle between the two rows of bars. The problem is they didn't follow the assembly directions, mind you all they needed to do was connect the three separate pieces.

I roll the directions into a cone and press them against the store owner's chest. "Read next time!"

His ragged beard moves with his mouth. "The pieces don't fit. They need to go back but the store opens in two days. I don't have time to wait on them to fix it!"

"I'm not a builder, but I can read. According to the directions the bars go in before you connect the pieces. Now you'll have to take it apart, put in the bars, then reconnect them."

The store owner grumbles under his breath as he opens the rolled directions. "Some help you are."

My aggravation rises to new levels as I storm out of the store and take a deep breath. This is an example of the frivolous chores we are assigned. It seems an abuse of power, but there are no laws governing realm walkers and the types of tasks they are to be assigned. In all of the realms there are few laws relating to us. We are allowed to marry hybrids in most realms. It is the lack of laws and loopholes we are planning on exploiting.

Ryel front and center always. I can't stop thinking about her, especially since the other night. I debate for a second or two if I should attempt to see her and find myself in Canida. The familiar teal light of the inbetween matter dissolves as the portal closes. I stand on the empty street like a heartsick dummy staring at the bar. The last time I was here it had rained and she flicked water at me with magic and turned it into ice cubes.

I will my legs to move but they refuse. Nerves flutter like Aradian solaflies bumbling and bumping inside me. I don't know if she's willing or wanting to spend time with me and not steaming over my sex refusal. A part of her must understand we are too young. There's only one guarantee the first time I realm walker has sex and that's followed with a baby.

The weather warmer than in Thraves, I drop the hood over my head, building up the nerve to go inside when she steps out, the door closing behind her. Her coat bulging awkwardly as she dances towards me, a smile twitching at the edges of her full, kissable lips.

Reaching me, she opens her coat and drops her eyes to the inside.

I worked myself into a frenzy worrying she'd never want to see me again and here she is, beautiful as ever, with my favorite drink stuffed into her coat. "Canidan Hops. Can you see inside my head, too?"

"No," she chuckles. "Only the realms, but I thought I'd snag a couple." She pushes her coat together and wraps her arms around my lower back as if nothing ever went wrong between us.

I wave a hand through the air, creating a door in the middle of the empty road, and my other arm I snake around her.

"Where does that go?" she asks.

"Open it and find out."

Her sumptuous lips curl into a smile. "Alright." Her soft hands take the knob and turn and her eyes twinkle under the starry sky as she twists. "Wow! What is this?" she asks, entering my inbetween room.

"My private world." I close the door and it vanishes.

She explores the items with hands and eyes running over the uneven tops and stopping at the pickaxe with the pearl handle and wooden axe head. She pulls it off its peg and runs a hand along the smooth pearl handle. "What is this?"

"It reverse harvests. The only one in existence."

She places it back on its peg. "Creepy!"

I can't take my eyes off her as she sits in my red chair and picks up the metal ball on the table. "Are you some kind of collector?"

"Sort of."

"What about this? Don't tell me it holds soul spheres." The ball resting in the palm of her hand.

I smile, walking closer to her. "It reads the future."

"Yeah." She squeezes the ball. "It's telling me," she drops the ball on the table and lifts her shirt over her head and throws it at me, "that tonight we are spending the night doing everything but."

I kneel on the floor and fold my arms around her waist. "It's never wrong."

She kisses my neck while her fingers find my abdomen and climb up my chest then pull my shirt over my head and drop it to the ground. She twists herself backwards, her full butt against my chest and pulls her leggings off. She takes my hand and presses it against the flesh between her legs. Her skin soft and supple under my fingers.

One hand explores her chest while I trace my finger along the magic spot. I drop my mouth to her skin and run my tongue along her taut abdomen.

"Look before you partake."

What? I move my hand away and lift my head, a tiny black lightning bolt catches my eye. "What is that?" I ask, trailing a finger over it.

"It's my lightning. I was born with it."

It is a perfect bolt of lightning. I kiss it, my lips lingering on the special mark, different from any I've ever seen.

My shirt and pants come off and she stands, thrusting her arms around my neck and her legs around my waist. I steer her toward the shelves, kissing the flesh on her neck and collarbone. "You're incredible," I say, the words spilling from my mouth like hot, sweet liquid.

"Don't quit what you start, always finish."

Her lips hungrily meet mine and the heels of her feet push into my back as we drop to the floor and I learn there are many ways to finish without doing the deed.

19

Hackey ogles me hard. "What's up with that goofy smile? Did you and Ryel...?"

"No," I rebutt instantly, "and its none of your business if we did." It was a night I'll never forget. We did many things, many times. The smile is warranted, but the conversation isn't.

"Don't jump down my throat. We don't need any little realm walkers running around right now but there's stuff, lots of stuff, you know that you and Ryel —"

"Stop," I urge. The hard wood chair is of little comfort and the conversation even more so as we wait in the lobby of Tuck &

Sons. One of the most esteemed architecture and building firms in Canida, run by a family of hybrids. It isn't obvious any of them are hybrids with so little elf blood running in their veins, unlike Ryel who is a wonder.

"Cyrus and Hackey," Tuck's eldest son Benny says as he approaches. "I think you'll like what we started." He continues talking as we stride to a conference room. "Shopping, condos, my favorite is the round government building in the center." He closes the door behind him.

On the table is a blueprint of Provence City. In the center is a round building. There are two main roads. One that passes a two-story shopping mall labeled Provence Square, large enough to include stores from every realm and specialty. The round dome building in the center is labeled Provence Hall and across from the mall are condos.

Provence isn't large even with my expansion, but condos can provide plenty of living space for those who live in Provence City. "What's this?" I ask, pointing to a large, unfinished building near Canida's curtain.

"A school for all children in any realm, regardless of pureblood or hybrid status. I call it Provence Academy. The city must be friendly for all. We show them by including, not excluding." His bushy eyebrows lift as he smiles wide.

That's it. Include. Provence was never a place for a single subspecies, but all.

He turns and grabs a large, folded paper from a shelf behind him. "This is the inside of Provence Hall." He points at various parts of the interior and explains.

The hall is circular and contains a caucus room for each realm including Provence. They can be accessed through the hallway that winds around the interior of the inner circle. Three rows of benches curve around the periphery of the inner sanctuary, with an empty floor in the center. Above is a dome ceiling. His idea is to paint the open realms on it, as a reminder of the goal we are working toward – unity.

He flips through sketches. The outside has several large, thick steps that lead to double doors. The structure is grand in its simplicity. I study the draft of the city. Thick trees, not the small double row that exists now, blocking the city from the curtains. As a realm walker I see through the curtains as though they don't exist, but purebloods see a reflection of Provence in the curtains. Hybrids, I'm not sure. I imagine they see the realms they are part of, except Ryel who sees them all even through my shield. I haven't figured that out yet.

Hackey stares at the blueprint of the city in awe. "This is more than I imagined."

Benny tucks his thumbs into his waist band and bellows his thick chest. "That's why we are the best." He leans towards me. "Hybrid vision and ingenuity."

"How many homes will the condos hold?"

"Eighteen hundred units, but we are thinking we could add another unit back here." He points to the space between an end unit and the trees. "They'd have the best view."

Eighteen hundred units is more than large enough for the current hybrid population but we need room to grow as others will come, seeking asylum. It is hard to tell how many there are. Some pass and will stay, such as Tuck. "I think that's a good idea, and to designate other areas where we can build in the future."

We talk more over lunch then Hackey and I depart, our minds filled with hope for the future. I'd never envisioned it would go this far. In a city of hybrids, it is only a matter of time before more Ryels exist – natural born realm walkers. Damn, I can't get her out of my head.

The lieutenant's voice booms in my head like a commoner bomb exploding. *Report now!*

I am about to get reamed. The tone in his voice tells me all I need to know and most likely it's the job from yesterday. I don't care.

Let him yell, scream, and throw a fit. I am over the useless tasks and jobs they send me on.

The teal light dissolves as I knock on the lieutenant's door. He thrusts it open, his wild beard covering his chest. He doesn't include any niceties. "I got a job for you. Don't mess it up! Your attitude is weakening the relations we've built with other realms."

"Most of the calls are an overreach. We are realm walkers made to keep peace between realms not solve everyday problems because one realm won't communicate with another."

His squinty eyes narrow and steam practically billows from his nose and ears. "The queen of Navarin has requested you."

The queen? What does she want with me? The fae are one of the subspecies that keeps almost everything inhouse and I'm not their realm walker.

Navarin, land of the fae, is covered in sparkling lavender seas. Islands with light green sand of all sizes dot the sea. Fairy dust twinkles in the air, carried by the gentle breezes, and trees with large floppy leaves offer little shade from the grueling sun in the golden sky. Born in Thraves, it is much cooler year-round. Even in the summer it doesn't reach the temperatures of Navarin in the winter months.

The energy in the realm is the most annoying of all. It feels like a million bugs crawling over my skin and insides. Combined with my nerves, I'm a mess. She didn't call me there for a friendly visit. She insisted we all join her. Every young realm walker.

The white palace is built of bleached sand bricks held together with fae-engineered cement that makes them nearly weatherproof. On the other side of the island are the mangroves. The thick trees and canopy of leaves make it impossible to see into them. They are mysterious and a place fae don't go.

Two guards stand outside the palace gates. Portalling into the palace is impossible as the heavy fae wards prevent it, not to mention how it will look. Not that I care a whole lot, but the fae king and queen are realm leaders and anything against them will reflect badly on all realm walkers, hybrids, and my home realm of Thraves.

Minding myself, I follow the guard past the colorful tropical gardens, up the wide, white brick steps and into the lower level of the palace. The floor is made of smooth marbled stone mixed with shells, and pictures of past kings, queens, and their children fill the walls of the foyer and spread into a great empty area with more pictures of royalty spilling into other rooms.

The guard's shoes clack against the floor as he marches toward the staircase. It spirals up a flight, the banister circling around. I've never been in the palace and can't keep my curious eyes from wandering. There are no doors, only arched entryways leading to other parts of the palace that I can't see. We reach the top of the flight of stairs carpeted in a lavender rug. Glancing up, I note the ceiling designed with molding, balconies on either side.

He goes left towards the ocean then up a smaller flight and through an arched doorway. Everything in the palace, including the moldings and railings, is trimmed in ornate precious metals. Not an expert, the light golden hue tells me it is probably trellium. A rare Verboten metal. I wonder which realm walker had to work the deal for all that.

The guard moves under the elaborate entryway and into an open-air room overlooking the sea. A steady light breeze sweeps over the area and cools my heated skin. One end houses a waterfall that drops from the ceiling and flows down uneven levels, puddling into a pool below. In the middle of the room are several chairs made of woven thick, flexible branches with soft fluffy cushions.

A table made of the same weave with a glass top makes the area elegantly cozy. The other realm walkers my age stare at me, including Marilisa. They've been waiting. Their comicay chatter unfiltered.

This isn't a friendly chat! Marilisa declares.

They know. We are dead in the water. What do we do now? It's your fault. Their voices are a symphony of doubt in my head.

The queen and king can't do anything without the court agreeing, Shiane says, as if that makes a difference.

You think they'll take our side! Jine asserts, her voice filled with anxiety. She's right. The fae aren't our friends and will destroy us if they can.

We don't know anything yet. Let's calm down, hide the fear in your faces, and see what she wants. It isn't a simple task hiding my own anxieties, but with all of us here it seems more of a diplomatic call.

I warned you! Marilisa says privately in an accusing tone.

I ignore her. There is no evidence the queen knows anything and Marilisa knows nothing, as she hasn't joined the fray.

The tapping of heeled shoes echo over the stone/shell flooring as the queen enters. A servant in front of her with a tray filled with dainty treats, seven extravagant teacups and a teapot. The servant places the tray on the table between us.

"Welcome to the White Palace. Please accept my hospitality," the queen says in a syrupy voice as she gracefully sweeps the back of her airy dress to the side and sits on one of the woven chairs. Her blonde hair is tied up in a braided high bun as elegant as everything else in the place. Her eyes blue and bright as a sapphire, framed in her dainty, heart-shaped face. Of all things evil, she is fiendishly attractive.

The fae are a divided subspecies and it works to their advantage. The current royal line are land fae with the incredible ability to transform into unicorns. Their horns are capable of remarkable magic. In the lavender seas are the sea fae or mer folk with poisonous scales, and in the air are the sky fae or sylphs. Their wings colorful and bright they also have the ability to spit sea water from their mouths, similar to dragons with fire or ice. The colors in their wings are said to confuse their enemies in war time.

The lavender sea twinkles beyond the rail of the balcony and from our vantage point the disturbance is visible. A whirlpool between the White Palace and Verboten. The calm waters of the land swirl downward into the depths of the sea. It isn't known what causes it, only that it's similar to the other mysteries in each realm.

Water laps along the shore beneath the balcony as the queen makes sure we each have a cup of tea. I'm not about to drink anything from Navarin. The fae specialize in spells and potions. I warn the others not to partake but Shiane, defensive of her realm, assures everyone the tea is safe. I let my warning stand. Marilisa, who thinks she's safe, takes a sip along with Hackey and Shiane. Lamont and Jine are more reserved.

Her shoulders square, back straight, and head held high, the queen is regal. The epitome of royalty and exactly what one might picture when they think of a queen. "I've called you all here because it is a fae custom to welcome the young generation of realm walkers. It is our ancestor and the blood sacrifice from a member of each realm that made you what you are, and your services are invaluable."

Is it a custom? My mother never said a word about it.

"It is an honor my queen," Shiane says. I hold in a gag. This woman is queen of her realm but I'm not sucking up even if the power in her horn can cause me to spontaneously combust.

"We want you to enjoy the day at the palace, explore our gardens, the beach, and have dinner in the great dining hall with the King and I this evening. Will you accept our invitation?"

She is good. Born into the royal line, she was groomed to be queen, and the king a member of the nobility of the realm who own businesses and have great wealth. In Navarin, the title passes from the woman to her daughter and only to the eldest son if the royal couple bear no female heir. The current king and queen are young and so far childless.

We have no choice really but to stay and we all have better things to do, except maybe Shiane. She's quite taken with the queen. They let us roam the palace and grounds freely. It is outside, through the gardens at the edge of the beach many meters from the palace and prying ears, that we are able to speak freely. Marilisa, Shiane, and Hackey all pile into a scrambler – an underwater vehicle. They hold four, including the driver.

Jine, Lamont, and I stroll the grounds at the farthest edge possible.

"This is all too convenient," Jine says. The wind pushes her shoulder-length, layered hair over her small face. She brushes the strands back and pushes them behind her ears.

"I think she's onto us. Maybe trying to smooth things over before the protest takes place, like if they can suck us into their royal web and fine lifestyle we won't do it," Lamont says.

I agree one hundred percent with his evaluation. It is possible this is a tradition, but the timing seems all too conspicuous. "The energy here is nipping at my flesh."

They nod their heads in agreement. "I have no idea how Shiane does it," Jine says as she rubs the shivers running along her arm.

Nearly everything is in place and I don't have time for this little vacation day to the most nerve-racking realm of all the middle realms. Suddenly, middle realms sounds off. They've always been called that and Lols is the outer realm, but is there a lower realm? If so, I'd never seen it, so why are they called the middle realms? In all my studies and objects hidden in the inbetween I've never found an explanation.

"How are you with transforming?" I ask. The other realm walkers are so unaware of the true power of their connection.

"Transforming what?" Lamont asks innocently.

Jine's eyebrows lower in confusion telling me all I need to know.

"To hide your appearance. If things go south, way south, you need to be able to hide."

Their eyes meet, as they never thought of it before. I need to teach them. We worked on shielding, energy bubbles, blowing energy out and bringing in it. Portalling is about the only thing they were good at.

Dinner is formal. They have us clean up and offer clothing tailored to our body styles that fit like a royal glove. Hackey, Lamont, and I wear matching shirts, fashioned in traditional fae style, made from soft fabric that's light against our skin. Tails fall over our rear-ends and long, skin-hugging pants cover our legs. We look like fae rejects. Lamont is so thick and burly the body-hugging tights do him no justice. Hackey nearly falls out looking at himself in the mirror. "We really have to wear this stuff? We look like ancient fae wannabes."

Shiane bubbles in the airy fae gown. Layers of fine, light fabric float over her legs and the top exposes her shoulders as it hangs over her chest and the tops of her arms. Jine and Marilisa don't seem as overwhelmed with joy as they take their seats at the long table made from smooth rock, swirls of color displayed in the grain of the rock. A mural of the first palace in Navarin covers a wall. The first palace, a haunted place of rubble, along with the mangroves are places fae don't visit. I can only imagine the treasures on that island.

Merla's grimoire. I'd never searched the whole island, it could be there or in the mangroves. Nobody knows where it is, or if she destroyed it so no one could repeat the spell that made us. Opposite the mural is another open air balcony, see-through curtains sweep across the floor with the breeze.

The several course meal is served with the finest Navarin wine, fermented from the sweetest kikans, a small, round, pink fruit. I don't want to eat in fear our food is laced with fairy dust and spelled, but I don't have much choice. I know enough fae hybrids now that maybe they can tell me if I get fae-bitten. A term we use when anyone unknowingly is spelled by a fae. Maybe they can even reverse said spell.

The evening culminates with a parade of servants bearing a gift to each of us. Once each gift is placed on the table, the queen rises.

A graceful smile sweeps her fine features. "Open them."

I'm afraid of what I'll find inside. Carefully, I lift a shell out of the bag. It is the size of my hand and glows in various colors. Every realm walker receives one.

"These are shells of noblest, a creature rare in our seas. When you lift it to your ear you will hear the call of the fae."

Don't! I blast the others. This is the spell, I'm sure. How thoughtful of them and conceited to think we all want to hear the call of the fae. They're worse than I pegged them for.

Shiane glows brighter than the shell, as if given the most supreme gift. Heeding my words, she quickly lowers it and thanks the queen. My shoulders roll in relief.

It's probably harmless, but I'll do some tests, she assures me. I'm not taking this gift to my inbetween world, but dropping it at my room in my parents' home, at least for now, or maybe I'll put it under my mother's bed. I change my mind. My dad sleeps in there too, and I don't want harm to come his way. I find a better place in Crest, under Blood Falls on the Thraves side. The queen can listen to large volumes of commoner blood sing to her.

20

My work training the realm walkers is far from finished. In Provence I teach them how to chain portal, meaning we connect our magic and portal to one location from differing locations. I don't exactly know where it will be, but aim for a remote location in Lols.

Ryel has no sense for portalling, unlike the realm walkers who are naturals. Her strengths are their weaknesses and their weaknesses are her strengths. Ryel rides with me.

Her face lights up like all the stars in Thraves as the teal light dissolves around us.

"What a rush!" she exclaims, pressing a kiss to my cheek.

The experience isn't strictly for her pleasure and awe, but an attempt to teach as I show her how to open a portal. Within uncountable portions of a second we are standing on snow-topped mountains spreading as far and wide as the eye can see. It reminds me of Thraves but with more trees and less white, powdery, cold fluff.

"It's beautiful," Shiane exclaims as she spins in a circle soaking in the views. "I never thought Lols was anything like this. I always imagined—"

"Something like Drakonia. Desert and heat. Getting banished here doesn't seem so horrible," Lamont interrupts with his vision of how he imagined Lols.

Shiane pinches her face. She doesn't much like being interrupted.

Jine offers her two cents as she wraps her coat around her middle to retain heat. "I always imagined it cold, icy, thin, hard to breathe air, and barren."

That is something else they needed to learn. "There's no need for you to ever be cold or hot. Imagine the perfect temperature and let it flow around you."

Jine's eyes round like saucers. "I never knew to do that," she states as she closes her eyes and lets the warmth inside and over her small body.

Ryel glows adorably in a fuzzy blue sweater and tight, stretchy leggings. "Now that you're all warm and toasty, it's time to figure out transformation. As a wolf it's a little different, I think, at first. Our bones snap and reform." Shiane grimaces at the thought and a visible shudder runs down her spine. Ryel continues without breaking her beat, "The first shift for us is the hardest, mostly because we know it's coming but don't know when. It's a shock to our system. After that, it is much easier because our wolf wants to come out and play, so we let it."

Within the blink of an eye, Ryel shifts smoothly into a white wolf. Her golden-green eyes contrast and stand out like light, golden-green tourmaline lying in pristine snow. She makes it look simple. I know for a realm walker it isn't and our change is more of a glamour than an actual shift, but I hope her experience can help them because I'm as empty of ideas as an opened bag of commoner cheese puffs, and losing my temper won't help.

Hackey surprises me as he quickly changes into a gray wolf with little problem but, as the Canidan realm walker, I can't say I'm shocked. He's probably seen the shift a million times and has a lycan parent. I have a natural tendency to transform into a troll. No idea why, since my family line are harvester hybrids and Drakonian.

With a scrunched face, Shiane focuses hard as if constipated, her eyes on something distant in the tree. After a few moments, her body morphs into a tiny animal with a fluffy tail. I can't hold in my laughter.

"Stop laughing you oaf!" she shouts and I double over in laughter as it keeps rolling on.

Lamont clicks his tongue. "You're cute," he says, his belly shaking as he erupts in laughter.

"At least I transformed," she snaps, sticking her head into the air. She makes a point. Lamont hasn't yet, and with dragon blood similar to Hackey with lycan blood, why not? He's seen the shift, has a parent that shifts.

Lamont and I laugh harder followed by everyone except Ryel who wears a stern, grumpy face.

"She's right, at least she did it. Look at the rest of you." Hackey moves to her side. He is larger than her, but not by much.

I clear my throat and push away my laughter, taking a deep breath. It felt good, better than good. "For us. I think it's a little different. I imagine what I want to be and spread the energy throughout my body." Within moments I transform into a troll then follow that with a wolf. "See."

It takes some doing and hours of patience before all of them are able to transform. It might be innate to me, but is work for them. Ryel is in full control of her wolf and races through the mountains. It seems almost more natural to her than her human form. Her paws light and nimble as she dashes through the forest and stops, her ears perk and eyes focus on something. I stop with her and follow her cues.

A house, a large house. Four stories high, vines stretch and strangle it. An overgrowth of plants, mostly weeds, swallow the base. My curiosity piques and I run faster than Ryel, passing her and around the side of the structure and stop. Its shape is something like a U but the sides more diagonal with five arches in front, behind the arches is a veranda and thick double doors. Dirt and moss cake in the bricks, telling me stories of its age, but the style says more. I know a little about Lols architecture and times, and my guess is the building was erected circa 1700. Cupolas hold windows on the fourth floor and several chimneys stand erect from the rooftop.

Ryel joins me, padding slowly toward the front arches, her head turns as she absorbs the splendor of the mammoth building.

A pointed block sticks out from the white, powdery snow several meters from us. With a paw I push the snow away, revealing a rectangular stone cracked in two, half of it smashed and weathered with age the other half reads 'Academy' in calligraphic writing.

Realm Walker

Immediately, I think of the academy Tuck & Sons is planning. Joining Ryel, I force energy towards the front doors. They open. She glances towards me then steps forward and enters. Dust and stale, musky air saturates our senses. She wrinkles her nose and I let out an irritated cough.

The foyer leads to a floating staircase and elaborate banister. I envision the academy filling with hybrids and purebloods together, learning and exploring their magics.

We continue through the entirety of the academy. My mind capturing every detail. The throat tickle disappears. Under the stairs is a seven-sided room and I think it's perfect. A side for each realm. A corridor leads to small rooms I think are perfect for offices, with their simple design and lack of closet space. A cafeteria, an actual outdated cafeteria, opens to an overgrown courtyard and gymnasium. I see plants, colorful leaves, and flowers everywhere.

The second floor has classrooms and the third floor houses empty dorms. The fourth floor is a large, empty space with endless possibilities.

Footfalls and chatter echo through the building as the other realm walkers catch up. I send my thoughts and images of the school to Denny. He doesn't respond right away. Shiane's fluffy tail hangs over the banister as she perches her tiny fluffy body on it.

Ryel brushes against me and tiny sparks travel to my core. *What are you thinking?*

I wasn't sure yet. The school has possibilities but the thought hadn't completely materialized. *What do you think?*

What a waste.

I nuzzle my chin over her head. *We can use it.*

21

I toss, turn, and flop like a fish without water. Every detail of the protest moves through my consciousness and refuses to shut down or even slow down so I can rest. My blood pumps and races through my veins. I think of the school. Denny likes what I showed him and thinks he can use it for the academy. On the edge of my mind there is something else, something lurking like a shadow, darkening my thoughts.

Tomorrow the realm leaders will wake up and hear our plea, our demands for equality. There can be no hitches.

A male voice speaks into my head. I've avoided him for months and don't welcome the comicay intrusion now. He's the last person I want to speak with. *We must meet in Provence. Now.*

I pull the pillow between my chest and the arm of the chair, ignoring him. There is nothing he can say that will stop me. Vampire blood runs through my veins. No doubt Preston knows everything. He is their realm walker and, at the start when the idea was fresh, I invited him. He chose to stay out. Why now? *Now!* he urges.

I close my eyes to push him out of my head. *Cyrus, this is important.* He annoyingly persists.

Pushing my pillow aside. He isn't going to let me pretend to sleep. With a frustrated release of breath, I pull on a pair of jeans and throw on a wrinkled T-shirt. Provence is always the same temperature, no need for a coat. It's against the rules to portal to Provence and against realm walker code, but heck with it. I can perform level 3 magic where others can't. Opening a portal, it appears then vanishes in the center of Provence.

Preston isn't happy with my portal, evidenced by his scrunched nose and narrowed eyes. I shrug it off. "What do you want?" I say with bite, wanting him to know I'm annoyed.

"You can't go through with your plans tomorrow. It has to stop."

I scoff, "It's too late for that."

"At the jeopardy of hundreds of thousands of lives?"

Where is this coming from? He supported me, privately. What happened between then and now besides my avoiding him after learning he is my father? "We want only what everyone has."

"The realm leaders are already scared. They've seen your power. You exposed every realm walker when you expanded Provence and formed the geyser. This hasn't gone unnoticed. They are beginning to conspire against us. Their egos won't let beings more powerful than them dictate the realms. Hybrids have long been feared because of their unique abilities."

So that's it, cold feet. He can't stand with us publicly and the geyser wasn't my doing but Ryel's. The first night she pushed the dirt away with her power and the water under pressure spewed upwards. I don't mention that. "It's time for a change. We have no plans to bring harm, merely make our demands known. This isn't a war, it's a protest."

"It must end or you'll make life unbearable for all of us."

"Join us then," I suggest, not for the first time.

"You are aware of who you are. If that gets out the realm leaders will destroy you first. They believe a union between two realm walkers that ends in offspring has double the power and strength. They have long feared us, which is why we stay silent. I have no children and will never bear another realm walker. It is impossible. Your actions will bring attention to this. It's no secret to M'ra as she's aware, has been aware. We keep no secrets from her. But the other realm leaders mustn't know."

Is he protecting me? No, he's salvaging his secret. The piece about an offspring with two realm walker parents, there is no evidence to it. The idea is ancient and the only merit it has is that as a realm walker ages it has less connection to magic. The child absorbs the energy and so it is always balanced. I am absorbing both my father's and mother's which explains my early awareness and innate skills – my connection is stronger, but am I stronger? "How do you think you'll keep that one a secret?"

"We are a haven for hybrids. It is the vampires who are in charge of banishing them to Lols. For those who choose to stay, we offer them a home. In their contract, they must never leave Drakonia or it will cause war between the realms. Not a physical war, but a war of trade. No realm can survive on its own. We need each other. That's what realm walkers do. They bridge the gap."

I read between the lines. "Are blood samples part of that contract? Is Drakonia searching for a hybrid of each realm?" I jeer. It is genius really. "A realm walker to fill your shoes. Don't try and be a father now. I have one and he's a better man than you."

"I understand how you feel about me. Come with me to Drakonia, meet with M'ra."

No, he didn't! He has no idea what it feels like to be me. I scoff, "She isn't more powerful than I am. No vampire is."

The light of the static stars shines on his hair giving it a golden hue. "It's not about power. Hear her out. She is the oldest being alive today and existed before the realm walkers."

"Fine." She won't talk me out of anything. Sure, she remembers the wars, but with or without realm walkers, the veils exist. Wars won't happen again and if they do I'm not to blame. My mind is made up, but I'll listen to M'ra.

I solved it! Shiane's words flow into my head. *If we hold the shell to our ear they can hear our thoughts.*

Fantastic! I knew the fae couldn't be trusted. Their precious shells are tools to spy. I alert the others to put their shell somewhere that will throw the fae off. Mine rests on a shelf under Blood Falls where I hid it when I returned from the White Palace. The queen can listen to the voices of the dead.

22

Drakonia doesn't look much different at night as the sky is always crimson red, shielding sunlight and moonlight. The buildings in Drakonia are modern, with sharp edges and darkened glass. I follow Preston through the doors of the tower and into the elevator. The glass tube ascends to the highest floor, splashes of tan sand and crimson sky offer dreary scenery. It's this moment I'm glad I didn't grow up with Preston. Thraves, even though Drakonia's neighbor, is filled with color, sunrises and sunsets, green plants and varying shades of wildflowers and berries.

Realm Walker

The elevator rises high and higher into the sky. As it stops the doors whoosh open to a long corridor. It's more inviting than the outside, with a burgundy runner over the polished wood floors. The metallic blue hue of the walls shimmer under the recessed lights.

From a distance, I spot two vampires standing rigid outside a door at the end of the hallway. They appear like small statues from a distance, like two vampire nutcrackers propped up for décor, and seem to grow in size as we near them. One is a man whose body is nearly the size of the door, a jacket buttoned over his bulky chest. It's muscle bulk not fat. I don't think he has any flab. The buttons holding in his hulking chest puff out as though they might pop any second. His eyes flash yellow. I guess he's a cat.

All vampires have increased speed, agility, and senses, but differ in their unique talents. Some portal, others mind bend and mind wipe, and yet others transform into beautiful large cats with mega sized teeth and claws.

A female in a dress suit stands beside him. She's tiny, not much larger than Jine, but size in a vampire can be their strength instead of a weakness, mostly because they don't intimidate. Increased speed and agility is a gift of a second life, and the smaller a vampire the more nimble and cunning. She is a pint-sized deadly force.

The door opens as if enchanted and the male moves his bulk to the side to allow our passage. Preston stops and takes a stoic spot next to the female vampire. *He isn't joining me?* I remember he didn't last time, either.

I assume guards will be inside the room, too, but they aren't. I'm alone and take the liberty of flopping onto a soft burgundy sofa as I wait for the holocall. The fabric is a delight against my skin and the stuffing molds my frame. I don't wonder long or think much, when I realize I'm not alone.

A tiny woman stands in front of a long, wide window. *Did she portal?* No, I would notice the light. No, she's been there, silent, creeping, waiting. It is the slight rustle of her dress when she turns that catches my attention. Her face, covered with a veil, is angled at the door and I sense her eyes staring at the guards who quickly close it. *I'm alone with M'ra?* A pint-sized deadlier force than the one outside the door. Rumor has it she only allows her most trusted advisors alone in a room with her.

I don't take my eyes off her, nor do I speak. If this is her, the holocall hid her size just as the veil hides her face. A red satin dress hugs her delicate, proportionate curves. The veil is shimmery gold, different than the one in the call. I wonder how many she owns. Do they hang in their own closet? Why does she hide herself? It isn't a secret, yet has no answer.

"It seems we have a lot to talk about," she says, turning towards me. The red silk flashes under the lights. Our eyes lock. I feel her piercing stare through the fabric of the veil and a shudder runs up my spine.

All I can think is: *no, we don't.* I have no business with her other than Provence and I don't feel I need her permission for that. "No, we want Provence. That's it."

She strolls to a chair that's a perfect match to the sofa I've flopped onto. I don't straighten or cower to the woman. She doesn't sit, her fingers mold over the backrest. "I don't blame you for your actions, nor the hybrids for theirs. I am willing to agree to giving you Provence. It was created with realm walkers and seems just it should belong to all of you."

What? I'm boggled. If that's how she feels, then why am I here? Does she want to help…? I erase that thought immediately. M'ra does what's good for Drakonia. She won't give unless there's a catch.

Her voice is almost sing-song as she speaks, "Drakonia has long been a safe haven for hybrids. It isn't their first choice, but many have come here seeking asylum, which I grant in most cases. But I don't make this decision lightly or alone. The other realm leaders must be convinced."

I don't get to black mail her? It's almost disappointing.

She chuckles lightly.

I'm intrigued and confused. I expected…I don't know. A fight. Yet she's giving me the green light to take Provence. I wonder again, why. What's in it for her? Is Drakonia overrun with hybrids? My tongue twists as my brain sorts. I can use her. "I have the help of many, now I need the help of the leaders most empathetic to our plight. I am your future realm walker as well as Thraves'. All the other realms will know of my parents' little dalliance, but I can give you a realm walker. A natural born realm walker." Not that Ryel is mine to give. She'd have to agree.

She pads around the chair and sits proper, with her legs tilted to the side. "I don't need a realm walker for Drakonia, although I'm interested in this one you say is natural born."

The cocky edge in her tone tells me more than perhaps she wants. My brain links the pieces. I never bothered testing the blood running through my veins, but I don't need to. I always knew, I think, or suspected. There's only one more ancient and powerful than the others, only one, and I'm stuck in a room with her. "You. It's your blood running through my veins."

She nods and doesn't attempt to deny it. "A single drop. I have seen, heard, and felt what you have, but only in flashes." Immediately she changes the course of the conversation. "I was a child in the time of the great war. The fighting spread like an infectious disease through Sier and Canida into Aradia. Navarin was frozen into an icicle by ice dragons. Verboten was a hotbed of politics and unfriendly to their enemies as they sided with the lycans. It all started when the dragon king's son grew ill and it ended with the dragon king's death and the creation of realm walkers. The veils stopped the wars and brought peace, but it has been hundreds of years and we have progressed no further."

I straighten at her confession. It isn't a shock, but I can't fathom why she's confiding in me. What does she want? The thought twirls and spins in my head. "You aren't against us." Her words and sincerity tell me that and I feel stupid stating the obvious "Why do you encourage us to stop?"

Pressing her elbow on the arm of the chair, she runs a finger over her manicured nails. "The first generations of realm walkers had work to do, starting with rebuilding the realms, setting up cooperation between realm leaders and starting the day trading in Provence. Each generation's vision changed, but nothing else changed once the purebloods were comfortable. Instead of protesting, start with conversations with the realm leaders."

There's value and wisdom to her words but her tone hides her true intentions. Her words are smooth, emotionless. I shake my head. "Our protest is peaceful."

I feel her eyes drop to her lap. "It isn't the realm leaders you need to worry most about. Purebloods are inferior and they know it. By keeping a strangle hold on realm walkers and hybrids they feel powerful. Protesting will remind them they are weak. Their connection to magic less than equal to yours."

That's why I've worked with the other realm walkers, teaching them all the ways to use their connection. I don't think any will be harmed, yet better safe than not. They need to learn.

Her eyes lift. I sense them on me more than I can see them through the veil. "This won't end the way you want it to. Someone will die."

I expect some amount of discomfort and even violence, but death? Murder isn't common in any of the middle realms. The meaning behind her words doesn't hit me in that moment. Even if everything she says is true we are peaceful, our protest isn't a riot. We have no weapons.

She sighs with a shake of her head. "For an incredibly powerful, charismatic, intelligent, and skilled realm walker, you are young. Rethink your plans and call on the realm leaders to meet you half-way. If you have their support, everyone will be safer."

No, the queen of Navarin already attempted to spy on us with shells. What are the other realm leaders planning? "Thank you for your support." I stand, without giving her another glance, and walk to the door.

23

Hundreds in each realm wait for the go ahead to march, signs ready and chants prepared. Hybrids and realm walkers stand together as one. My heart races with excitement. As a group we are many and strong.

We are connected through our comicays, thanks to our dragon hybrids who tweaked the mechanism. We can see and follow each and everyone's movements. We can communicate without interference. M'ra's words leave me with a feeling of unease, yet I'm not backing down.

That's what she wants is for me to halt this. Preston too. They aren't really with us.

Anyone not with us is against us. What all the realm leaders want is for this to stop and life to return to how it was. I ignore that tickle in the back of my brain that maybe she's right. No, I won't allow her to manipulate me. I don't answer to her. I answer to the gathering crowd.

I don't march in Thraves, leaving Kini and Jerry in charge. Light spreads through the gray clouds, golden streams touching the midlands of Thraves. To me it is a sign.

I don't march with Ryel either, who volunteers to lead the march in Drakonia. A wolf in the land of vampires, I didn't coax her, but can't help smiling at the irony and hope M'ra is watching. I know she will from her penthouse perch in the tower.

Ryel, able to take care of herself, is perfectly safe in Drakonia. Not a single vampire will go against M'ra and I'm learning vampires aren't exactly what I thought. They aren't savages, even though they live in a savage land. They are progressive and refined, yet live under a dictatorship. Vampires are most perplexing.

I've chosen Aradia, as Marilisa refuses any part of the protest. I remember my vow to manipulate her into it but never followed through, any more than having my blood tested. Aradia has the largest number of hybrids in any of the lands and I wonder if they outnumber the purebloods.

We gather in the Karank woods
outside the capitol in Aradia. The realm is
breathtaking with its dense woods, trees
splashed with silver leaves. Flowers populate
every area, vining trees, hanging from leaves
and bushes, and bunches spring and pop from
thick tree roots.

Marilisa is nowhere to be seen,
meditating under Serenity Tree I imagine. I
don't understand her obsession with it, nor do
I care. With or without her we'll have
Provence. She can camp under it permanently
for all I care. Build a trella or elf home near its
moat. The hybrids and realm walkers are
united. I make the call and we march into and
through each capitol.

Purebloods watch, some with disgust
on their faces, others smile, yet others are
unsure. A few raise their arms in support of
our protest, others slink away into their
businesses and homes in an attempt to ignore
us. I walk side by side with elf hybrids.

Through each realm, we march
towards Provence. Chills of joy raise the hairs
on my arm. In Navarin they protest outside
the gates of the White Palace and I wonder
what the queen is thinking. In Verboten, they
march through the futuristic streets of
Rubina. Tears well in my eyes. It's happening.
I don't fight the sensation of freedom. I let it
move through my being. I know this is only
the beginning and it's happening. Really

happening. I wonder if the commoners who marched through London felt what I feel.

Ryel and the hybrids in Drakonia march unfettered by any vampires and in Canida they march bravely past growling purebloods. In the caves of Sier they march. The tears teasing my eyes fall on my cheeks. I can't remember a time in my life that I've cried. We did it and without the violence M'ra predicted. Most protesters follow us in as we march through the curtains into Provence, crowding the marketplace. I brush the tears under my eyes.

I stop, halting the crowd, our thoughts spreading through the hybrids' upgraded comicay design to halt the march. In the center of Provence, purebloods gather from every realm except Drakonia. I don't fear them or their feeble magic as I approach, but I do remember M'ra's warning.

A tall, thick lycan with a square face sneers at me, his voice booming through the small area. "You have made a mistake! We will not back down so you can take over our realms!"

"We don't want your realms. Keep them!" I scoff. "We only want what's ours."

More purebloods taunt and jeer, but none as loudly. They are small in number and we are many. We stand as one. I take the hand of the hybrids to my sides and we raise our arms. Others follow like links in a chain.

Hackey joins me, puffing out his chest to appear larger than he is. His eyes studying the square-faced lycan, but no words escape his lips. It is more of an intimidation thing. I'm not sure who's doing the intimidating. The lycan is by far larger and bulkier than Hackey.

"Realm walkers and hybrids. You are atrocities and we never should have let any of you live this long," the persistent, annoying, square-faced lycan shouts. He stands no more than a few feet from me. A few other lycans behind him, standing with him, and a fae to his side. His words dripping in ego and self-importance. Other purebloods raise their arms in agreement.

I meet his steely gaze. He may shift into an ultra large wolf but I can portal him to Antarctica alongside the hunter who shot an arrow into my back. "If anyone destroys realm walkers the realms will fall and life will perish." I throw in the last part. Merla's words, according to history, don't say life will perish. They imply war will replace peace, but eventually that leads to death. I improvise.

He scoffs, some of the others back away with my warning as if suddenly remembering we are off limits. In all the centuries realm walkers have existed no one has ever attempted to harm one.

"I fear no silly fae curse!" the lycan shouts above the roar of the crowd.

REALM WALKER

The fae standing with him steps back and away from him with his toxic speech. They understand the power of level 4 magic and the bond between blood and sacrifice. A blood spell can't be undone without more sacrifice. It is the strongest of all spells. Fear flashes in the fae's eyes as the implications of death turn their stomachs. They know. It was a sea fae who created and implemented the spell.

Lamont and Hackey grab a leg each and hoist me to their shoulders. I see above the crowds. I hold my hands into the air. The curtain to Drakonia opens. Its red sky gleams over the heads in the crowd and Ryel steps into Provence. Her golden-green eyes glow as they do before a shift. She marches through the day traders and crowd of onlookers and doesn't offer apologies. Her shoulders square and chin up. Purebloods step back, allowing her passage, and join the shoppers and traders.

She is magnificent and commands an audience. Her eyes radiant like stars and determination painted on her face. There is no one like her anywhere in any realm. She stops in front of the giant, square-faced lycan and orders, "Go!" through the pointy tips of her wolf fangs.

That single word carries through Provence and the lycan lets out a low growl.

I'm sure if he could shift, he absolutely would. shift that she is mightier than him.

"This isn't over!" he threatens through gritted teeth and marches away. For him, I'm sure it's not. He'll return to Canida and stew.

24

Most of the protesters go home, our voices heard without violence. Now the real work will begin. It is time to call on the realm leaders. We have no plans to forcefully take anything. We want what is rightfully ours and a pact that will help all the realms. Other than M'ra, all the realm leaders have been silent.

I don't fool myself into thinking they aren't calling on each other and in communication. I'll wait, we'll wait, but only for so long, eventually our patience will run out. Ryel and I lie on the grass near the geyser, looking up at the static fake stars.

"It's like your world, an illusion that looks and feels real," she says, our hands clasped between us.

I rise and settle on my side, running a finger along her face. I correct her, "It's no illusion. It is real, encapsulated between the realms, Provence is carved from each realm. If I take away the protective barrier in the sky the sun would be harmful to the vampires."

"Get out of here!" she quips.

I twirl one of her braids between my fingers. "I don't want you going home to Canida tonight." I don't fear the lycans, any of them, but I don't want her in harm's way. In Canida, the lycans can shift.

"What are you proposing?" Her golden-green eyes meet my gaze, trapping the twinkles of the stars over Provence.

I lean my head down, our lips touching. "We celebrate in my world, and after I'll teach you how to build."

Her words lost between our kisses, her hands gently tugging the Aradian band that holds my hair off my shoulders. It falls, dropping over her chest. My hands explore her curves. She arches her back and out of nowhere a low growl escapes her lips. Not a moan of pleasure but a menacing, threatening growl. I'm caught off guard as she lifts up and slides away from me, her body shifting into a black wolf. The change so smooth and quick I admire before I think. She leaps over me.

Realm Walker

Everything happens so quick, quicker than my mind processes it. Her form, a shadow in the darkness, vaults feet into the air, front paws extended, forcing something to the ground. Her jaw opens and her fangs sink into flesh. I see a form beneath her struggle. She screams. It's filled with pain. My heart thuds in my chest. Whimpers hollow an area between my ears and brain and I watch her lycan form return to human. A shining rod in the center of her chest.

Time slows as I press my hands over the grass to stand. My hand brushes something hard, narrow, and long. I recognize its form. An arrow. My eyes take in the shiny silver arrowhead. She shifted to save me – us – going after its shooter.

In a moment, I'm running and dropping on the grass beside her, holding her limp form, a dead lycan by my side. His square face stares blankly in my direction. The flesh torn in areas, hanging, and deep grooves from her sharp predator teeth mark the gap in his chest. A wail explodes and echoes through Provence before I realize it belongs to me. The agonized sound wave moves through the atmosphere.

My cheeks are covered in wetness as I pick up her limp body and hold her in my arms. Tears drop from my chin to her face and slide off her cheek. She blinks, ragged breaths move her chest. The shining rod is an arrow in her heart. I press my head to hers. "Don't talk, save your energy. I'll fix this."

"No…it's too…late." Her chest heaves one last time and stops.

"I love you! I'll fix this. Don't give up." Tears mingle with my choking scream, sending a deafening sound wave through the realms. "No!"

My only thought is to get her to Drakonia. Their blood can save her. A swoosh brushes over my skin as a poorly aimed arrow whizzes within centimeters of my head. Through my realm walker vision I see three lycans gather, their heat a target in my vision. I gather energy and shield us. Arrows hit it and ricochet off.

Crushing their bones is my first choice, but that won't be enough for a lycan who spends a lifetime perfecting the act of breaking every bone in their body and reforming them.

I lay her body on the grass beside my feet and raise my hands into the air, lifting each lycan. Their feet dangle above the earth. I squeeze my hands together and choke their airways. I hear their rattled breathing. I squeeze harder. Warm blood coats my palms as my nails dig in.

A force freezes the energy beaming from my hate. "Killing them won't bring her back," Marilisa's voice speaks from all directions. "If you kill, they will come for all of us. Death helps no one."

I push against the force, allowing my rage to coalesce. I loathe her self-righteousness and how she chooses to use her power against me. *Who is she?* They struck first. Ryel at my feet, rage builds. "I'll feel better!" I push again and squeeze harder, balling my fingers into my fists.

"You won't. The guilt will eat you up," Hackey's voice joins the chorus. I can't believe he's taking her side. He is more lycan than I thought. My energy focused on the lycans, if I shove at him or Marilisa I lose my grip on them.

Jine's words mimick theirs, "The laws of the realms will punish the guilty lycans."

They've all turned against me! Why now? Why do they choose to show their strength against me?! I empty the rage swirling in blackness and push against the realm walkers who seek to stop me. The lycans fall. Their chests working hard to fill their lungs.

Traitors! *Have they learned nothing of the laws?* "No, they won't!" My words explode with all the darkness inside me. It eddies and cleaves fractures in the veil over Provence. Small lines ebb into the other realms. Trees snap in their wake and seismic waves ripple through Provence, forcing the lycans through the curtain and pushing the realm walkers who fight against me alongside them. They puddle into heaps. Their power diminished as I collect Ryel in my arms and portal us to the tower in Drakonia.

"Help her!" I shout, in tears as the teal light vanishes. I stand on the shiny tile floor of the lobby.

Several vampires relax their fighting stance but don't say or do anything. "Help us!"

Preston emerges from his own portal. His hazel eyes meet mine. He steps in front of me. Is he going to help me, be the father he's never been? "It's too late. The window has closed," he says.

Not being the father. A father would fight with his child, he'd help save the love of his son's life even if it meant giving his own. I push wind at him and he stumbles backwards a few steps. "Act like what you are! Help her!"

My own sticky blood leaks from my hands, mingling with Ryel's. A female vampire licks her lips but doesn't make a move. She doesn't want to save her but drink her. A mixed hybrid, I bet her blood is a delicacy to vampires.

"No!" I scan the vampires. "Why are you staring?! Help her! Your blood can save her!"

The female vampire cautiously steps towards us, her eyes change from hungry to pools of sorrow, her voice concise but gentle. "She's gone. Our blood would only turn her now. She'd become like us. Take her to Thraves where her soul can be harvested."

My throat constricts and breathing becomes a task. It can't be. Their blood saves lives.

She speaks the truth. Harvest her brilliant soul, watch her sphere rise to Tranquility. M'ra's voice speaks into my head. She's a wolf. I can't turn Ryel into a vampire, someone who depends on the blood of others for life. All that she is would vanish. She'd no longer be the creature she is.

I bury my face into Ryel's chest, my own chest heaving, and portal us.

25

Teal light vanishes. I stand in my inbetween world, Ryel's lifeless body in my arms. Carefully, I lay her on the chair. Her blonde curls spring at her cheeks as if she's still alive. Her dark cheeks hold their natural flush, but her eyes stare toward the ceiling. No twinkle or sparkle. Her full lips don't curl at the edges.

I may not be a harvester, but I know what they do and how they do it. Growing up in Thraves, I know enough. On my knees, I allow myself to think for a moment that she's only sleeping. A slumber she'll never wake from. Running my hand over the soft curls on the top of her head, I kiss her cheeks, wet with my tears.

Hanging on the wall is a pickaxe, its old wood handle smooth from many years of use. I stole it as a child for the sake of adding it to my collection of precious magic toys. I suck in a deep breath mottled with anguish and my body shudders. Ready, I swing the axe into the air and lower it to her forehead. A string of deep violet light stretches above her, coiling in a ball.

I move the head of the axe upwards and guide the soul. The violet sphere rises high into the room. It looks nothing like her. A soul, powerful and bright. The color of her light shows how strong her connection to magic is…was. Not washed out like the hybrids in Lols. It's deep and radiant like a star. It ascends and I gulp as it disconnects from the axe. Soon she'll be gone, and the thought of never seeing her again, holding her in my arms, our naked bodies touching, tortures my soul, twists it into something I don't recognize. A part of me I've never accepted.

The deep purple lights reflects on the pearl handle of the reverser hanging on the wall. It won't bring her back in physical form, but it can bring her spirit back temporarily. I drop the pickaxe and hold the ball of light in my energy grasp and fight Tranquility's pull. It can't claim her yet. I'm not ready. I know it's wrong. It goes against the harvester code, but I'm not a harvester. I'm a realm walker.

She isn't going anywhere. Tightening the walls of my world, I fight. My feet dig in and my stance straightens. Daggers of pain, sorrow, and rage merge into a dark force that eddies in the room. Shadows churn from the corners and join, gathering around her soul. They tug it downward.

No one can have her. Her soul isn't for the taking. I use every ounce of my energy to envelop her soul sphere. Noise like a swarm of locusts reaches a crescendo. Her soul hangs between two worlds; the living and the dead. The noise festers in my ears, gnaws at my soul and heart. "She's not yours!" I shout and give more and more until the pull of Tranquility stops. The room goes silent. I hear my own breath and carefully release the energy bubble I trapped her in.

The darkness melts away and the shadows vanish. I can't explain what happened. There isn't a book on my shelf that can offer any clarification. Somehow I kept Tranquility from taking her. A pit in my stomach forms, growing quickly. It fills with darkness. *What have I done?*

Grief is a powerful thing. I collect her body in my arms and take her to Lols. I understand why the commoners bury their dead, why they hold onto them with a vice grip. It is sorrow that fills me up as I part the earth about a meter from the Academy.

The gap is large enough for her to rest in peace. I lay her body in the hole, kiss her lips one last time and, through the tears that blur my vision, I cover her body with dirt. There will be no headstone to mark her grave, no service to see her off, only flower petals of my love as I drop them over the turned earth. They spin as a chilly breeze kicks and carries them into the air. They weave and bob, spiraling on the breath of wind, through the mountains, the tiny petals spread pieces of her throughout Lols.

To be continued…

HEART OF DARKNESS

Suggested Realm Walker reading order:

These reading orders are suggestions only. Try one out or find your own.

Enjoy the Ah Ha moments (order written by author)
In the Shadows
The Land of Lost Souls
The Origin: Marya's Journal
Hidden Passages
Soul Fire
The Ring of Betrayal
Heart of Darkness
Soul of Malice
Life after Death

To thoroughly enjoy the HFN
In the Shadows
The Land of Lost Souls
The Origin: Marya's Journal
Hidden Passages
Soul Fire
Heart of Darkness
Soul of Malice
Life after Death
Ring of Betrayal

The prequels can also be read first and Life After Death last.

SOUL OF MALICE

Sneak peak!

The light dissolves. Lamont is standing in the middle room of the trella, his thick chest heaving with each breath. Shoulders rising and falling. He turns to me. "I can't believe you! I'm here because of you. My family isn't safe with me there and now they probably aren't safe with me here! You have no concern or empathy for anyone else but you! Always you!" he says, his voice rising with each word.

I've never seen him like this. Didn't know this side of him existed. "I have family too. My mom and dad are in Thraves. They're in as much danger as yours!" I hurl the words at him.

His fists ball and a whirl of energy smashes into my chest, lifting me off my feet and driving me backwards into the wall. My breath expels and the picture to my right crashes to the floor, shattering into tiny, sharp pieces that scratch my pants, tearing holes and poking into my legs. I'm impressed with his strength.

He marches at me, arms lifted slightly at his sides. My lungs labor for each breath and I don't have the chance to defend myself before busy, nippy energy encapsulates me. Lamont's hand moves from his side in front of his face and I slide upwards with it. He controls me like a puppet. "Everything is going haywire and you just keep…doing…all the…things that make it worse. Nothing you do makes it better. They'll go after our parents. Did you even give a moment's pause to consider that?" His brain struggles to put the words together.

My airways are breathing now. Not normal, but improved. The power behind the energy blast was incredible. I admire it. Admire his anger and blooming strength. It was always in him. "Yes," I say in a strangled voice. "I'm leaving here…" I pause and suck in as much air as my thrashed lungs will hold. "We aren't safe. We have to demand they give us Provence. They have no choice now." I pause for another lungful. "Don't you see? No one is safe, not you, not me, not our families, not even Marilisa, but we can mend the veils. We can use that."

The angry energy surrounding my body doesn't let up and I don't fight it. "You don't even hear yourself." He shakes his head.

"I thought we were friends. You have no friends. When I told you about Hackey, you shrugged it off. No big, who cares, he's the lycan realm walker. I'm going to get him and I don't need you!"

His words slice the sliver left of my heart. The consuming energy dissipates and I slide down the wall, landing on the same pointed fragments of the picture and my already injured tailbone. It jars, and ripples of sharp pain move up my spine and neck.

He stomps away toward his room shouting, "I'm not returning!"

The door bursts open and Marilisa's petite frame seems to tower in the doorway. Her eyes flashing pools of red heat. She doesn't wait to be invited, slamming the door behind her. The tapestries on the wall rattle and slant sideways.

Hands at her sides, her chest heaving in and out, pulsing with the rhythm of her flaming eyes. "The tree is dying, veils are ripping, wolves are invading Drakonia, tensions are rising and the lycans are holding Hackey." She thrusts an arm with a pointed finger in the direction of Canida. "And the two of you are—" Her soliloquy stops cold as she studies my precarious position on the floor and Lamont's scowl. He looks like fire might explode from his mouth at any moment, bringing the entire trella to a pile of singed dust.

"I'm going to get Hackey. You coming?" he asks her.

"Absolutely!"

My lungs are breathing normally now and I pull myself up. "Not alone," I say.

Both glare at me. I'm really glad neither breathes fire. Lamont walks past me, ignoring my presence, and opens the door. The sarcanthum flowers shine bright and solaflies blink in and out of the flora.

We blink through teal portals into the center of the legal capitol of Canida. It's not like Johnston's Pass with cozy wood structures and a view of Sier's highlands. Wide steps made for large lycan feet ascend to tall brick buildings reaching into the sky. Lights brighten the streets, and the prairies Canida is famous for don't exist in the metropolis.

I contact the lawyer through our comicay. His response is quick. *I'm on it. Paperwork is done and they're bringing him out now. Don't do anything hotheaded.* His head voice is calm and all business.

I can't promise the boiling cauldrons with me won't try something stupid but I'm gentle as a Navarin seabreeze, mostly because every part of my body, including parts I wasn't aware of, ache and burn. In the past week I've been inhabited by a wraith and icy magic from the scythe, beaten, battered, and bruised.

Realm Walker

The lawyer's voice speaks in my head. This time it's not settled but shaken and almost condemning. *They're accusing him of murdering three lycans. The three you tried to kill in Provence, but there's no bodies.*

This stabs me straight in the heart. I've hated on Marilisa, Hackey, and Shiane for their betrayal yet skulked in my room instead of enacting my vengeance. Someone else has stolen that glory and satisfaction of watching them squirm and beg as they die an agonizing death.

Marilisa taps a foot, arms folded across her chest, lips drawn so taut small lines cut into them. "What did he say?"

"That he's got it under control and not to do anything hot-headed."

Lamont lets out: "Pfff…you not do anything hot-headed." He shakes his head and paces, walking past Marilisa then back.

Seconds stretch into centuries as we wait at the legal square. Marilisa's foot tapping like a drumstick, back to me, and Lamont paces six large steps forward, turns on his heel and six steps back. Lycan lawyers scuttle past us and I count the number of pedestrians.

Marilisa's hair reflects silver from the light of the moon, with shimmers of pink and blue from the stars blinking in the darkness. I shift my gaze to the steps and will my mind not to watch them.

Several more minutes pass and I see Hackey and the lawyer descending the steps. My aching body and the palpable tension, I'm overjoyed when they approach. The hybrid lawyer wears a dark suit, his shoes shiny as the stars. White light reflects from them with each step.

Lamont stops his pacing but Marilisa's foot continues to pummel the ground beneath it. "He can go home for now but is expected in court on Day 1." In Lols that would be a Monday. "The lack of bodies won't keep him safe in the current political climate. I need evidence."

"I know people in Thraves," I say.

Hackey doesn't say a word until after the lawyer leaves. Lamont and Marilisa smother him with conversation and she wraps her arms in a hug around him. A twinge of emotion pings in my dead heart. I lost Ryel and have been to the Otherworld and back, my body thrashed, and I got anger not hugs. Jealousy. The annoying pang is jealousy.

I wait, contacting my connections at CIU. I know the purebloods won't lift a finger to help him but the few hybrids will.

Hackey steps beside me and leans to my ear. "You'll find what you want beneath Provence. There are tunnels."

My brows lower in surprise. "You—"

He cuts me off quick, holding up his hands. Silver bands wrap his wrists. "I can't leave Canida and they took my comicay." I don't think the silver will hold him.

Shock and disbelief tremor inside me and settle comfortably into respect. He didn't kill them, but put them somewhere no one but a realm walker can find them. It's clever and devious, but the comicays will be a problem. I don't know how long we have before they find the chip. Our communication is compromised.

www.ingramcontent.com/pod-product-compliance
Lightning Source LLC
Chambersburg PA
CBHW030909200726
48289CB00003B/954